"Normally in literature, it's qui[t]
support protagonists who comm[it]
these two do, but Fields woos the reader into the characters' court
quite successfully."
Windy City Reviews

"*Homo Superiors* is a fascinating examination of the psychology
of the criminal mind that achieves its effect by reimagining
the notorious killers Leopold and Loeb as modern day teens.
Particularly impressive is how Fields evokes the mood and tone
of early Brett Easton Ellis, giving us two highly intelligent boys
whose lives have been made vapid by privilege. As one boy becomes
addicted to criminal acts of ever-increasing magnitude, the other
finds himself a willing pawn, drawn into the scheme out of a
frustrated same-sex desire. *Homo Superiors* offers complex insights
into the darker aspects of a friendship where no one is innocent."
**Sean Eads, author and Lambda Literary Award
finalist for *The Survivors***

"L.A. Fields stuns with her latest novel, *Homo Superiors*, in which
she modernizes America's first 'Crime of the Century,' the infamous
Leopold and Loeb case. *Homo Superiors* is a gripping and shocking
tale, but a murderous obsession I enjoyed reading and I know
others will as well."
Cina Pelayo, author of *Loteria*

HOMO SUPERIORS

L.A. FIELDS

LETHE PRESS
MAPLE SHADE, NEW JERSEY

Published by LETHE PRESS
118 Heritage Ave, Maple Shade, NJ 08052
lethepressbooks.com

ISBN-10: 1-59021-626-1
ISBN-13: 1-59021-626-1

Editor: LAYLA BYRD

Cover and interior design
by INKSPIRAL DESIGN

STRANGE BIRDS

1

STUDENTS BLAST FROM THE DOORS of the law building and into the quad like buckshot from a rifle. It's Halloween weekend—zombie makeup and drooling vampire bites are already painted on some of them, witch and cowboy hats bob above several crowds, candy wrappers sift down from the clusters of people to blow in the wind like autumn leaves.

Noah can't get away from them fast enough. He's hurrying out of a test he knows he did excellently on, despite what the professor called his "troubles at home" when she offered Noah an extension. His mother had been sick forever—for the sixteen years or so since his own unfortunate birth, in fact. Her death has been a long time coming; it is not enough to make him choke on a mere Ethics test.

The rest of his classmates are buzzing about their weekend. It'll be all cold-flicked nipples under skimpy costumes, pumpkin beers and hard ciders, bonfires guarded by the relatively sober so that nobody falls in trying to roast a marshmallow, all of it the kind of fun they came to college to find. It'll be just like the movies, and they all look so revoltingly happy about that.

"Noah!"

Noah closes his eyelids for a brief moment before he turns around, to give himself a little privacy while he rolls his eyes. There's only one person (professors included) on this entire campus whom he holds any positive regard for, and the peon shouting at him now is not the one; Ray never bellows across the quad like a cow in a field.

"Hey, Noah, you'll be there tonight, right?"

"No," he says to Tucker Bolton, a new pledge in Ray's fraternity. "Be where?"

"The ZBT Halloween party!" Tucker is two years older than Noah, but nothing about his presentation would broadcast that fact. Tucker's wearing pajama bottoms and a hoodie, while Noah is dressed with all the fastidiousness of someone used to wearing a uniform—he's been in private and prep schools his whole life, and even out of jacket and tie he's buttoned up and belted. There are enough future politicians and lawyers in their pre-law classes that it's Tucker who stands out, not Noah, at least in their manner of dress. Some people are part of a herd no matter what, and some people always stand out.

"I can't go," Noah says. He wasn't officially invited, first of all, and besides: "I have a funeral to attend." Everything in the courtyard behind Tucker is in a bright, dying, autumnal rapture. The ivy growing up the face of the law library bleeds scarlet at the tips. Most of the trees are half-bare already, but the ground around them is covered in firework bursts of orange and yellow leaves, like confetti at a celebration.

"Yeah? That's cool, which house is doing a funeral theme?"

"My house," Noah says snippily, and he waits for Tucker to begin saying, "Yeah? Where did you pledge?" before cutting him off with, "My mother died, you simpleton."

"Oh, I'm sorry about that, man," Tucker blinks at Noah from beneath a University of Michigan ball cap—he's only been a student here for a few months, but already he's wearing the school's colors like he feels a total belonging. He probably does belong here, feels it all the way to his bones and never questions it. Noah came here following Ray, and for what? Ray wants to find his own friends, and be a Zeta Beta Tau, and drink so much he C-minuses his way through every class. Noah has never felt any allegiance to this school.

He turns to walk away from Tucker, uninterested in the dimwitted fallout, when the guy calls to him, "Hey, you don't have to be mean about it though! My grandma died last year, I know how it is. Seriously, you shouldn't alienate your friends!"

Noah casts a withering glance over his shoulder and continues to walk a swift clip back to his dorm room. Noah doesn't have any friends. No one but Ray can even pretend to tolerate him, and Ray too is starting to slip away. Ray, who is the only person Noah considers anywhere near as smart as himself. Ray who knew Noah's mother, and used to charm her into a smile even when she couldn't muster the strength to get out of bed.

Noah's headed home to Chicago tonight, so he can be there for the funeral tomorrow. Stepping from the afternoon chill back into his dorm room—a double that's only occupied by a single since Ray moved to the ZBT house—Noah slumps briefly in his soldier-stiff desk chair to wallow. His bags are packed, his bus ticket printed and resting on top of his heaviest coat, both items accented by a long cashmere scarf his mother got him last Christmas. Ray never gets over the fact that Noah refers to it as canary like she did, instead of plain old yellow. Every time he wears it, Ray makes a crack about sending it first into a coal mine.

Right now Noah wonders if it's enough scarf to hang himself.

2

RAYMOND'S MOTHER WOULD BE SO ashamed if she knew how her son spent his time.

There are a lot of ways to cheat at cards. The easiest ways involve the trust of amateurs—robbing your buddies can be simply done with a glass table and a dropped card, or reflective surfaces behind their heads: a clock face, a china cabinet, the opacity of a turned-off television set, or the mark's own thick eyeglasses. On the next tier of difficulty comes your own slight-of-hand: stacking the deck, dealing from the bottom, throwing down two cards and picking up three, or the classic ace up your sleeve. But the most effective robberies involve a two-man crew, a partner. Ray has only had one of those, but Noah's *persona non grata* at ZBT if Ray wants to stay a member (and he does).

Ray has exhausted the basics without Noah around. Sunday night of the Halloween weekend, ZBT is playing a quiet game of low-stakes poker. His brothers are hungover, either stung or satiated from last night's girls, and everyone is slowly sipping a gentle bottle of Hair Of The Dog, no one truly drunk, but each one far from sober.

Ray, with his tried-and-true boringly amateur methods, loses two games on purpose, wins one in what looks like an accident, and then loses again before nabbing a full pot on the fifth round. His brothers just throw their cards down on the spill-tacky kitchen table and let him have all their laundry quarters without a fight. The boys roll out of their chairs and slump up to their rooms without even cursing Ray's 'good luck.' They suck the joy right out of Ray's masterful maneuvering. Ray counts his winnings without relish or pleasure. Seven dollars and seventy-five cents, an insult.

Ray decides to take a walk. He goes up to his room, trickles his money into the glass vase he uses for change, causing his roommate to groan and roll over in protest, but not wake up. Saunders over there has already thrown up twice today, each time he tried to peck at a little food. He'll be sorry clear 'til Tuesday, and he'll probably never drink tequila again.

Ray slips on his loafers, pockets his phone with his left hand, and swipes his hair back with his right. He's seen leading men of his same slim build do that in movies and has copied it consciously, practiced it so that it comes nearly naturally to him now.

He takes the stairs two at a time, a bit of a skip on the last, a bounce out the front door, and steps lively down the drive. There are several fraternities on this uneven block of streets—the Phi Gamma Deltas, the Delta Gammas, the Gamma Alphas, the Alpha Phis, the Alpha Sigma Phis—all quiet after the holiday debauchery, all essentially the same to Ray. Last year he decided to rush for fun, but after the surprising welcome from the older guys (much older— Ray too is only sixteen, going on seventeen) and getting friendly with them, it became obvious that joining a house was the smart move. Noah followed him around so much that rumors erupted, insinuations were made, and boy if people didn't just *hate* him. It was more than Noah's greasy hair and insect eyes, more than his sneering tendency to lecture everyone on everything. Ray was reading the room constantly, trying to reflect back what he saw and succeeding, but that meant he could see people tighten up when Noah lurked into the room. He was an unsettling stone in a cool pond. He made shoulders hunch away from him in waves.

It's not really his fault, the poor sport. He's the smartest person Ray ever expects to meet, but you need a little verve in this life, a little social grace! Noah doesn't have an ounce of it, and Ray forgives him for that, but he can't have it rubbing off on his own shimmering self.

Under the dim fire of a fall maple tree, Ray brings out his phone to call Noah. The call is answered instantly.

"How was the party?" Noah asks.

"It was a party," Ray says, swinging around the stop sign at the corner of Oxford and University, like Singing In The Rain. "I just won thirty-seven dollars and seventy-five cents at cards though."

"Oh, really? Well, if we're telling lies, then I believe you," Noah says.

Ray smirks, assuming that Noah can hear it when he says, "How was your thing?" He admits nothing, but he does like to give Noah a nod occasionally, credit due to someone so astute.

"My thing was dull and a nightmare," Noah says with a sigh. He sounds stretched out in bed, shoes off but socks on, intending to get up in a moment to change for the reception downstairs, but unbuttoning slowly now to the sound of Ray's voice.

"Any hysterics?"

"No, not for *my* mother, not with how long this took. Mostly everyone squeezed me and gave me that look, you know? That sort of pained fart, we-won't-be-surprised-if-this-screws-you-up-forever-look, like they've just lowered their expectations?"

"Can't say that I know that one, personally, but I get what you mean." Ray stoops to pick up a few rocks as he turns the next corner, his walk taking him just around the block. He tucks his phone into his shoulder and starts trying to nail tree trunks and mail boxes along the way. "Hey, when you get back, what d'ya say we work out a new routine for cheating at cards? Find a poker game somewhere, or easier yet, host one."

"We can," Noah says. "We can do whatever you want, but I think . . . I think

I'm going to apply to go back to Chicago in the fall. It's not really my scene in Michigan, and besides, my family's here."

"So's mine, that's exactly what I like about Michigan."

"So you don't mind if I transfer?" Noah's voice is loaded, serious.

"I don't mind," Ray says, coming back to Oxford Road and approaching the ZBT house. "I do *care*, but you've gotta do whatever you have to do."

"Right." A sigh and a shift. "Of course."

"Don't hold it against me, okay? Whatever you decide."

"As if I could. I'll see you."

"Yeah, later."

Ray returns up the driveway and walks into the front room. The guy who drew sober-sitter last night—Tom Schwartz—is getting good and wasted by himself now, and watching some game he missed over the weekend. Normally the most recent sober-sitter hates Ray for a few days because, when drunk, Ray can be an instigator. But last night he didn't feel like participating. He accepts Schwartz's offer of a beer now though. It's some kind of seasonal cinnamon-spice travesty, but Ray can drink it without flinching. That was lesson number one when he showed up to college at fourteen—learn how to drink with the newly adult. Ray figures he could hold his own with his father's scotch-swilling business buddies at this point.

"Hey, Schwartz, you like money, don't you? How'd you like to help me work out a system at cards?"

"What d'you mean 'system'?" Schwartz frowns, his thoughts fuzzy with nasty leftover beer, his unibrow cinching tighter.

"Like we could work out signals so I know when to bet, switch off so no one gets suspicious, we could clean up around here."

"You mean cheat?" Schwartz sneers, revealing his uneven teeth. "What are you talking about? These are supposed to be your brothers; you can't just steal from your brothers."

Ray begins to laugh before Schwartz can finish his sentence.

"Well, can I joke with them? Man, you should see your face, you'd think I'd asked you to join a terrorist cell or something."

"Oh," Schwartz says, and then shakes his head through his haze. "Sorry. I forget that you're always joking around." He forces out a 'ha' that might have been a burp, and Ray slaps his shoulder and leaves for the backyard, where he'll sit until the sun sets.

Remaining above suspicion is all about knowing when to leave the room. Ray smirks and thinks, *To achieve true believing, I must be leaving.* That gives him real pleasure, and he grabs another beer on his way out to make sure the feeling lasts.

3

NOAH'S OLDER BROTHERS, MIKE AND Sam, are home for the funeral—it's convenient timing, but no one would ever use that word. Mike's been meaning to bring home his fiancé, but the first Hanukkah was given to her family, so it might have been months before they saw her without this. Lillian's exactly the girl their mother would have picked for him—smart but wants kids, pretty but doesn't emphasize it, with the strong but unvarnished nails of a girl who isn't shy about doing dishes the old fashioned way, and Jewish as all get-out.

Most of the guys Noah knows—cousins, classmates, Ray's fraternity brothers—everyone is dating goy girls just to piss off their parents. They won't do it forever. They know it, and so does everyone else. They don't want to spend their actual lives explaining food, words, and customs to WASPs, or listening to their in-laws trying to mimic the Yiddish accents they hear from comedians.

Noah's mother told her three sons: if you want Jewish children, find them a Jewish mother. The Kaplan boys will not even pretend to bother with any other type of girl. They have never picked a fight with their sick, sweet mother, not once in their lives. And their father? There is no fight left in their father either.

Dad and Mom's sister, Aunt Clarice, sit together on the couch. They were the ones closest to Faye since she became nearly bedridden after Noah's birth. Their grief is so exclusive and so dense that no one can approach them; the rest of the reception mills quietly about the downstairs of the house, atoms circling a nucleus.

Noah sits in a deep leather chair in the sunny corner of the living room (though it's evening now—the sunset a milky purple like a lavender-scented bubble bath), where there are book shelves full of popular fiction and magazines, the kind of reading material a guest might enjoy picking up. The law books are in his father's office, cookbooks in the kitchen, bird books installed in Noah's room, and every trashy crime novel Ray has ever bequeathed him in a box under his bed (like porn). Those books stink of Ray—of his cigarettes, the backseat of his car where they might have stayed tossed for weeks, his spilled drinks and flecks of food, the sweat of his hands. Noah keeps them all in one box mostly so no one going into his room will think he likes such moronic pabulum, but also so that the smell stays concentrated. When he's feeling particularly lonely Noah will stick his big, ugly nose in there and breathe deep.

"Here," Mike says, having walked right up to Noah without him noticing, holding two rocky tumblers of pale green liquid. "Have a gimlet, it was Mom's favorite."

"Really? You're going to hand me this right in front of Dad?"

"Come on," Mike says, patting Noah's shoulder and sitting on the arm of his chair. "You're in college, and you're bereaved. It doesn't matter how old you are, you're not a kid anymore."

Aunt Clarice must feel Noah's eyes on her, just noticing how much she looks like her sister—the heavy eyelids and dark hair that Noah inherited, the long neck and grace of movement that he did not. She turns to smile at her nephews, and when they raise their glasses to her, it's enough to make her lip quiver before she turns away again. Aunt Clarice never had any children of her own, and her husband died years ago. She's been a second mother to her three nephews, and to Noah most of all, the youngest, the baby.

The baby who's old enough for cocktails now.

Noah sighs and downs the rest of his glass. Ray would smile to see him do it, he's always trying to rope Noah into reckless abandon, but Ray's the sort of boy who will never lose anything unless he chooses to let it go, and that's not exactly fair. Ray's still got his *wisdom teeth* for heaven's sake, both sets of grandparents, good looks, and the sort of charm that could run for president. It's his privilege to abandon himself, with all that will never abandon him while he's gone.

And of course he's all the more irresistible now that he's grown tired of Noah, but it's time to stop following him around. Noah's mother would want him to have at least half the self-respect God gave a worm, so it's back to Chicago, for sure. Dad will be happier to have him back home, probably, and Ray will be relieved to get rid of him.

Everybody wins.

4

RAY DOESN'T SEE MUCH OF Noah for the rest of the fall semester. There are finals—which Ray makes about as much effort at passing as he does in showing up for them at all, while Noah always holes up for weeks reading everything twice and highlighting his own notes in an attempt at what the locals call 'studying,' though Ray rarely sees it in action himself.

Then there's all the hard work to be done for the sake of partying, and while he finds much rewarding in these pursuits, it does leave him with a touch of what his mother generously assumes is a cold when he comes home for the holidays. In fact, after a day and a night back home, even with a grandma and grandpa over, and a great-aunt whoever from Canada, and at least two of his three brothers all milling through the house, no one seems to think Ray's outrageously hungover. No one takes him aside for a talking-to at least, although that could be Ray's own careful trickery at work.

Ray resorts to several artful maneuvers to hide his delicate condition from his family. Here's how he talks himself through that first weekend back home:

First: plead motion sickness from the bus ride home so you can sleep it off a little longer.

Second: claim you're too tired for dinner tonight, and say, "Besides, it's better to save up space for the big Christmas feast!"

Third: thank whichever deity you'd like for the fact that this is a Christma-kah household—with a Jewish dad and a Catholic mom, they just throw all the best parts together and leave out anything too boring for the opposite-faith in-laws to tolerate; you know you couldn't sit through all that claptrap without turning green tonight.

Four: when the sweats break over you because you've gone and stood up too quickly, find something cool to casually lean against wherever you are—the marble of the stairs' chunky starting newels works, or a nice window encrusted with the snow outside, or the stainless steel of the refrigerator if everyone's standing around talking about the food.

Five: DO NOT put any of that food in your mouth or even stand too near those dizzying fumes.

Six: if you're hungry you can be forward-thinking and smuggle some crackers and water into your room (and try to get those in you right before you fall asleep so you don't have to deal with digesting them).

Seven: spend some time thinking about which bathrooms are farthest from your resting relatives while you're kept up by a vague nausea; you know, in the worst case scenario that whatever damage you've done is so profound that when you finally sit up, you have to rush to the bathroom to puke up that detainee dinner you just had, and wonder if its pinkish tint is just the color of stomach acid, or if it's blood.

Eight: the next day when it turns out someone did hear you vomiting in the night, and your mother's diagnosis of cold is upgraded to flu, and your father secretly offers you some warm brandy instead of medicine, quit trying to be a hero and just drink it.

Nine: the cure ALWAYS involves some touch of the curse, that's what science the boys at the house taught you, so just pace yourself this time.

Ten: and pace yourself the next time you know you have to be home in the morning, you're seventeen already and this is childish.

It's a trustful gesture on his dad's part to sneak him some booze, since even with his older sons he doesn't approve of drinking, thinks it finds weaknesses in men that might otherwise never be discovered, makes them lazy and complacent. He's so sure all his lectures over the years on alcohol have been heeded, he acts like Ray's never raided this cabinet before. It could be a wink-wink, nudge-nudge sort of thing, or maybe with four sons he never could know which one had been at it, and he just assumes it wasn't the young duckling who started college when most kids are starting high school. Maybe with his CEO position at Sears he just doesn't have time to notice what state his family is in unless they make him late for a meeting. Who knows, maybe the maids replaced the missing booze with water thinking they'd be blamed. Ray never spares too much thought to his extraordinary luck. It's tough to think critically about what has always been right in front of one's face, or at least that's what his sociology professor says.

"Don't tell your mother," his father says to him with a playfully warning smile. "Or her mother, or my mother either."

"I just won't tell any of the women about it, how's that, Dad?" Ray says, sipping carefully and wincing—he doesn't like the taste of brandy, and his throat is still a little raw from puking. His father probably takes it as proof-positive that this son isn't much of a drinker. Good old Mom and Dad: they're as generous in their high opinions of Ray as they are with their money.

"That's a good plan," his father tells him. "That'll serve you well when you get married someday."

"But not any day too soon, right?"

"That's right," his dad laughs. "You really are the smart one in the family."

Getting married, how Raymond shudders to think of it (or is that the cloying taste of brandy shivering through his body?). He never wants to get married.

He's having too much fun.

5

NOAH DECIDES TO FINISH OUT the year before switching schools. He arranges with the University of Chicago to have the classes transfer over, he plans to speak with a few professors at Michigan to make sure they won't forget him when it comes time to get recommendation letters for law school, and . . . he does hold some hope that Ray will come around to say goodbye.

But as his family's old driver used to say when Noah's parents weren't in the car: "Wish in one hand, shit in the other, let me know which one fills up first."

For months he waits. He shadows Ray's classes so as to glance him from both near and far. Noah reaches pathetically for metaphors as he lets Ray walk past him, surrounded by admirers: he's a lightning rod among weathervanes, a ball bearing among food pellets, a steeple among chimneys. It wasn't that long ago that Ray saw Noah the same way—not in the sense of coordination or looks or wit or anything appreciable to most people, but in superior thought and conception, in mental brilliance. Ray is brilliant in everything he's made of: a ray of glittering sunlight piercing through a dull, dim blanket of clouds.

But come April, Ray never manages to catch Noah's eye or feel his presence or think to stop by his room (that was the longest shot in all the world over anyway, but still Noah held out a shred of hope), and so it's up to Noah to stop by Ray's frat house.

Sure, they'll spend all summer in Chicago about a block away from each other, but who knows what kind of complications will erupt back in Chicago: old friends, family vacations, that strange tendency to regress when home from school that makes them both act like kids again, act their true age. Leaving Michigan feels like the end of something, a closing book. Noah wants to see him one last time before it's over.

He stops by the ZBT house, a testament to how necessary this feels, because he hates this place and it's no fan of him either. Or, not the physical place—that's irrational—but certainly the people in it.

"Here to see your boyfriend?" some bro asks when Noah steps inside. "We were worried you guys broke up."

Noah rolls his eyes and moves through the common area. The floor is scuffed and filthy, thinning linoleum under a flattened, dirt-grayed dorm rug. None of the furniture matches. Noah can smell the couch from across the room. Something black and viscous is oozing from the refrigerator door. The trash can is heaped as high as it can go, and is surrounded by a corona of fallen garbage. Noah tries not to even touch the walls as he makes his way upstairs.

Ray is assembled on his bed like a pile of spindly camp fire sticks—one knee up, one arm straight across it holding a bent-back book, one elbow crooked behind his head.

"Nice," Noah says from the door.

Ray smirks without looking up from his book. That's Noah's invitation into the room.

"I should be Basil Hallward right now, you look like you're posed."

"University Youth In Recline," Ray says.

His roommate's side of the room is empty, the cracked plastic mattress stripped bare, revealing the indelible white stains that all the school mattresses seem to have. Noah avoids them by sitting on the roommate's wobbly desk chair. Ray's chair is covered with clothes.

"Packed yet?" Noah asks pointlessly.

"Nope." There are clothes on the floor too, books piled all over—on the desk, the floor, on top of a stack of dirty dishes. School books mostly, but the collection is infested with his ubiquitous detective novels, and some few philosophy books as well.

"What's that you're reading?"

Ray keeps reading (or pretending to read) but lets the book's cover loose so Noah can see that it's *A Clockwork Orange*.

"That's a good one, no wonder you're so enraptured you can't look up."

Ray smirks even more and finishes a sentence (or pretends to, one never can tell with him) and finally sticks a scrap of paper in it and sits up.

"So are you gonna miss the place?" Ray asks, holding his arms wide enough to indicate the campus, maybe the whole state.

"Nope," Noah says back. "Maybe you a little, but not this place."

"*Maybe* me," Ray mumbles with amusement. "Help me pack."

He gets up and starts to separate out his things, and Noah—supremely disappointed in himself but unable to do anything about it—gets up to help. His one claim to dignity is that he makes Ray deal with his own dirty clothes and only touches the guy's books.

"Doing anything this summer?" Noah asks, trying not to wince even as he says it. This was supposed to be *goodbye*, but it looks like some poor bastard can't seem to help himself.

"Maybe," Ray taunts again. He runs a hand through his hair in a distracted way, though Noah knows he's practiced doing that, saw it in a movie or two, adopted it because he can get away with it. His hair is just the right length to stay where he pushes it, in a soft little wave above his ear. Noah's own hair is too greasy to touch much after he combs it down each morning.

"I'm going to keep up my birding classes I think," Noah says.

Ray whistles low. "My God, you know how to have fun, don't you?"

"Obviously I do, since I'm here helping your worthlessness pack for nothing. You haven't seen me once since my mother died, you know that, right?"

Ray freezes, then turns to look at Noah with a genuinely shrewd look in his eyes. The light from the window is cutting through one iris and making it glow like a glass of iced tea.

"Would you have really liked me better if I came running over to console you? If you ever tried to hold *my* hand through a tragedy, I'd never speak to you again."

Noah considers this just as seriously: did he really want Ray to be one more person in the endless single-file of the Sorry-For-Your-Loss people? Of course not. Ray's a lot more special for being the one person in Noah's life who didn't immediately infantilize him.

"I'd respect you for that, I suppose. Pity is contemptible, to give or receive," Noah says.

"I should hope that you'll always respect me," Ray says, going back to sorting. "It means more coming from you than from anyone else I know."

Noah smiles, but tries to twist it off his face before Ray sees it.

He suspected—he *knew*—that this wasn't really meant to be goodbye after all.

6

Ray's summer vacation starts out as boring as paradise. Two days of sleeping, one week in the pool or on the tennis court without a single thought in his head except *stroke-stroke-stroke*, and then a day of finally unpacking his dirty laundry and settling back into home.

In line with that tired axiom, Ray believes that a change in work is far superior to the mental stagnation of rest. He cuts back on his partying significantly just as the general herd begins to stir to the promise of summer in the city. Backyards and rooftops and lakeside lolling are what everyone will be doing—everyone who's home from school like Ray, and young like Ray, and of the moneyed unemployed like Ray. There's nothing so resistible to Ray as being just like everyone else.

He shuns groups over his summer, makes himself a mystery. He answers cryptically every message or phone call or shout from across the street that comes along:

A call answered: "Hey, Ray-Ray! Where you been all summer, man? Don't tell me you've got a job! You're too young to go out that way, man."

"Not a job, but several occupations."

"What?"

A text responded to: *We're doing a bonfire on the beach this weekend, and if you aren't there before midnight I'll throw myself on the fire, so be there or be responsible for my death.*

Try now, we can only lose.

What?

A holler returned: "There you are! Stop by this weekend, me and Eber have some girls coming over."

"Not the kind that'll be coming over any of us I bet!"

"What?"

"I've already got plans."

Ray has found people usually assume the best about him, the exact opposite of how they treat Noah. Ray says he's busy, and it's got to be some girl, some party so exclusive that no one'll ever hear about it, some lucky trip where the pictures are too scandalous to even *take*. He doesn't know why they do it, just a certain *je ne sais quoi* he must have, a mischievous spirit about him. Noah tells him he's puckish. Ray has warned him never to use that word around anyone normal, as it sounds filthy.

They're right in their suspicions, but entirely wrong in their conclusions. The real pursuit of Ray's summer is . . . pursuit.

There are only so many detective and spy novels a man can read before he starts looking at the world differently, before his movements become furtive and his eyes dodgy. Ray has been watching people for years—it started with a telescope from his bedroom window as a kid, an eagle-eyed vantage from which he could take notes about the comings and goings of neighbors, then he graduated to the more complicated art of watching all the other people on the same bus or train compartment. He learned how to look at people only when they weren't looking at him, to use reflective surfaces, to use an 'accidentally' dropped item to gain a better vantage—all skills he later tailored quite expertly to hustling his friends at cards.

But this summer Ray wants to do more; all that he's perfected has become boring to him now. This summer is his first and last in a way—he turns eighteen on the eleventh in this very month of June, becoming an adult in the eyes of the law, never to be a child again. He decides to embrace this change, and step up his game.

The way to learn how to follow people is to start easy, start with people in all your own brackets. For Ray that means young white males, the kind who dress nicely but not ostentatiously, because they've been brought up with rules for how not to get mugged. Next try older men, the kind who might be wary of any younger man as some new brand of thug.

A level harder: follow women of any sort, progress by following them in darker and lonelier circumstances without them becoming aware. They'll hunch and hurry like a rattled cat if they feel your gaze, and it's best to let it go after that; a lot of them carry mace or even Tasers.

Next level: get out of the suburbs, out of your own comfortable neighborhood, and try to walk and stalk unseen on the South Side, which turns out to be hardest of all for a boy like Ray. Suddenly he turns disturbingly visible; he considers it a valuable experience for gaining insight on his targets, but does not repeat this exercise.

And what is this all in preparation for? Nothing so far, just a natural extension of his curiosities. Ray can pick a few types of locks now, nothing too crazy, just household doors, drawers, and file cabinets, but you never can tell when a skill like that might come in useful. He'd like to learn how to get into parked cars at some point, just for some light marauding with purses or computers left under seats or people's toll booth quarters. Just enough so that they lose a little that Ray gains, just for laughs.

He gets home from these outings with lies for his parents, too, but complex ones. It's a litany supported with witnesses, the kind of lies that are half-true, gathered from all his other interactions:

"Dad, I know you want me to keep to my studies and not get a job, but what do you think about a summer internship? I feel a little useless."

"Mom, a girl invited me to the beach tonight, what should I do?"

"Tommy, you should get to know Eber's little brother—there will be girls over there this weekend. I would go but I've got this chick on the line . . . Mom keeps giving me advice, she might be that kind of girl."

It's *so easy* to show them all who they want to see. Lying should make him feel bad, that's what his old nanny used to tell Ray, but why should he feel bad about making everyone else so happy?

7

NOAH'S SUMMERS ARE A NECESSARY evil. With no classes he has time to read literature, to write bird articles and send them to the journals and websites he respects, and to plan his future with the same numbered precision that his father sets down when considering a new business venture. It's numbers numbers numbers. Three, possibly two more years until graduation if he keeps taking online courses. Five, maybe four more years of graduate study. One hundred fifty, maybe two hundred thousand dollars of his father's carefully accumulated wealth to turn his son into a lawyer, and then it'll be more numbers numbers numbers, because Noah plans to practice estate law and not criminal.

So his summers are needed: locked up and hot in his bedroom as he was during his sickly childhood, where he learned all this focus and discipline, where he learned how to learn for stimulation because he was never allowed out to learn from experience.

"Why birds?" people ask him when he is 'of the world' during the school year. Why would any man who isn't retired care about birds?

Noah never tells them the truth. Birds are all he used to see out his window that held any fascination for him. His mother loved them too, for the very same reason: the sick must love birds.

Noah's mother was fading for so long that they had time to finalize two wills over the years. She mostly had her good days when the weather was having good days. Noah was as quiet and present as she was growing up, and he knew some of her friends thought she was faking.

"Sick, sure, sick in the head," one murmured to another after a visit on a nice day, a day when Noah's mother had invited them for lunch on the back lawn.

Noah was a boy then, home from school because all the pollen in the air was stuffing his head with highly pressurized mucus. His head throbbed hard every time he blew his nose, and bright light made him squint and wince. Even so he had still helped his mother set up her table and makeup a bright complexion onto her face (Noah helped by blowing excess blush off her brush). If those women could see how pale she was underneath, or how it drained her just to get up and down the stairs, they wouldn't talk like that behind her back.

Then again, maybe they would. His mother always told him they were frightfully petty gossips.

Noah drops his glasses from his face onto the desk. His eyes feel like undercooked meatballs, and if he's daydreaming about his mother it means he's due for a study break. He takes his binoculars from the bedside windowsill and heads downstairs through the thick stale air that never leaves the middle of the house no matter how often they open the windows on cool nights, hoping to air the place out. Noah doesn't realize how oppressive the atmosphere inside has gotten until he finds himself blinking at the post-lunch summer brightness outside.

Now, the way to spot birds is to first spot where they are not, to find their ripples in the leaves. There is a slight breeze that makes the treetops sway gently, rhythmically, and if at any point a small section of leaves shivers against the regular motion of the rest of the branches, chances are there's a bird or a squirrel up there. Noah scans slowly with his own vision, allowing his sight to expand to take in as much area as possible. When one of the branches shimmies, its leaves rustling like the fringe on a dancing dress, Noah squares his stance and raises his binoculars.

Noah is scrutinizing the branch trying to rule out a possible squirrel, searching for feathers, for colors, when he feels a stinging flick on the back of his neck.

Noah assumes some bug has launched itself at him, but when he looks around for the offending creature all he sees is a rubber band in the grass at his feet. Then he hears snickering, adolescent laughter. Then he sees two boys on their bikes, one with a kitchen junk-drawer rubber band ball, the other with a crude wooden pistol meant for firing them at people.

Noah scowls and moves further away from them, closer to his neighbor's yard, and out of range of their gun. If they come onto the property, surely Noah's justified in braining them with his binoculars, right? How desperately he longs to. The boys continue down the street disrupting every pleasant thing they find: they send a rubber band into some jogging woman's frizzy ponytail; they send another into a rather pretty wind chime with colored marbles and wire curlicues, knocking it into the dirt; they send one at a mailbox's raised red flag, which leaves the flag crooked. There's nothing that they can't ruin.

The grouchy old bitch next door is out on her porch. Noah hadn't noticed her when he fled this way or else he would have just gone back inside. She used to glare at him something fierce whenever he was outside burning ants with a magnifying glass as a child, but now suddenly they are on the same side.

Their eyes meet, and she nods grimly toward Noah before saying, "If they come back around here you feel free to whip their little behinds with my garden hose, you hear me? The nozzle's nice and heavy." She nods next at the hose, coiled like a snake on one of her refuse bins. Noah nods back at her; they're coconspirators now.

Ray would like that idea, Noah and bitter old Mrs. Rosen murdering a couple of brats together, a little vigilante neighborhood justice. And as soon as that thought occurs to Noah, he turns and hurries inside for his phone so he can tell Ray all about it. He's been waiting for a good enough reason to talk to him again for what feels like forever.

If his trusty binoculars hadn't been hanging by a strap around his neck, they would have been dropped and forgotten.

8

RAY IS ON A TRAIN platform when he gets Noah's message, lost like he tends to get around trains, daydreaming.

What Ray wouldn't give to have lived just a few decades ago when trains were loaded with goods and money instead of just droolingly stupid commuters. He wishes he could be riding alongside a train, horse-backed and hollering, leaping onto the money car and putting the guard in fear of his underpaid life. Cracking a safe with a stethoscope, explosives with fuses held together by twine, a hat to tip up and down like a rearview mirror to do all a man's emoting for him.

That's how Ray sees himself, the way he truly is. If only everyone else could see it, too.

Noah's message says, *I found some candidates for murder. A couple of brats just rode by with a rubber band gun. Mrs. Rosen and I are going to beat them to death.*

Ray chuckles and sort of dandles his phone affectionately. Good old Noah, he always did know how to cheer Ray up. Too bad he never has that effect on anyone else.

Ray's train pulls up and he steps in, noting that it's the start of rush hour, so there are some few seats in each car, but they won't last past the next stop. In the midst of everyone tidying themselves into their own seat or getting a secure grip of the support bars for standing passengers, one grubby homeless man is taking up three seats all on his own.

His ass is planted in one, his feet are propped on another, and he's got an apple core holding a third seat open as he eats his dinner. Ray manages to sit across from this specimen of inferior humanity, and starts observing surreptitiously.

I've got a good candidate for murder too, Ray types into his phone to Noah. *This animal across from me on the L is taking up three seats when there are standing passengers.*

Christ, Noah sends back.

An apple core is keeping the seat next to him occupied. He's eating an entire Entenmann's cake with his disgusting bare hands. It's chocolate, so there's no telling if the lines under his nails are dirt or icing or a troubling mixture of both. What Ray finds himself typing next almost makes him sneer.

He's licking himself clean.

The man puts the empty cake box and apple core under his seat and lays sideways for a little nap.

He's using an old pizza box as a pillow.

Noah comes back with, *This is why murder is necessary. Mankind is a long way off from becoming Supermen with scum like that gumming up the works.*

Everyone else in the car is ignoring this man and his rude arrogance as hard as they can.

Somebody should kill him, Ray agrees, *but there'd be no challenge in it for us, no reward. No one would miss him and we'd never get a ransom.*

Good for practice?

Good for nothing.

Ray decides to walk his last couple of stops—he can't stand the congestion in the car, trapped and watching this cretin misbehave. It's just too depressing. It's about to spoil his whole young hopeful life.

Once he squeezes his way out of the car like some substance out of a clogged pore, Ray feels better. With a little space he feels free, athletic, acrobatic. He lifts and swings himself gently on the moving handrails of the escalator. Topside, out of the subway, he hops up on the edge of every stone planter he finds on the streets of Chicago, each one a balancing beam. He's come to the Loop in the early evening to do a little "Man of the Crowd" action, just roaming and roving wherever there are people. He likes to move through the shifting throngs with precision, a kayak through rapids, hands in his pockets, his shoulders dipping back and forth like a double bladed paddle. He challenges himself to anticipate which way people will break around him and to dance with them for a moment, never having one of those awkward face-to-face shuffles that ruin the waltz.

Ray's on the look-out for someone interesting to trail, but this being a weeknight, it's mostly just working folk headed home, harried from today and dreading tomorrow. They won't do anything overly interesting for Ray to see. After about an hour of this type, Ray considers ducking into a movie theater, putting his feet up in the dark, getting drunk off the flask of gin that's warm from being strapped to his outer leg beneath his right sock, and then taking a cab home to pass out.

But before putting that plan into action, Ray decides to walk one last wide circle out to Lake Shore Drive. It's gotten dark enough for Navy Pier to be lit up and beautiful against the sky, nice far-out Gatsby-grasping lights reflected on the lake.

Ray lands himself on a bench with a view of the pier's electric sweep to look up what movies are playing where, but before he gets too entranced by his phone, he spots a one-legged pigeon hopping along and decides to creep up behind it for a while.

He or she is a tenacious little thing, covered in a dirty city sheen, bouncing down the sidewalk with purpose. Ray turns on his flash and snaps a picture of it for Noah, sending it to him with a question: *Hey birdbrain, what do you think happened to this little guy's leg?*

Some alley cat probably took it, Noah responds, along with a second message a second later. *Or it got cut on some garbage, got infected, and fell off.*

Thanks, you're a font of knowledge.

Any time, my friend.

Ray abandons his bird after this, his curiosity temporarily satiated. He starts heading to the movie theater, thinking he'll just see any crap off the marquee, and also thinking that since Noah's now transferred back to the U of Chicago, he can afford to be nice to the kid again. He'll spend the summer being aloof, and beginning in the fall they'll be a whole state apart, and there won't be any harm in keeping Noah sweet on him from afar.

After all, he's still the smartest person Ray knows.

9

It's the first day of school. Again.

The best place for Noah to be is not in front of his full-length mirror, but it's an important step in the process to achieving perfection.

Slick down the hair so he doesn't have to worry about it moving. Belt the pants, not too tight, but tight enough so he won't have to fidget with them all day. Socks clean, shoes laced tight. An undershirt for catching sweat, and an outer shirt, whatever one his hand first hits when he reaches into the closet. He owns nothing but the same shirt in slightly different colors because he doesn't need to look interesting; he's no peacock. Noah feels better when he can't be seen by himself or by anyone else.

He must be in school, it's his true arena. He only wishes he didn't have to get there, or if only the commute would go much, much faster: down the stairs, hi Dad, no Mom (again); car, train, swarms of people (why); asphalt, stone steps, hardwood, desk (finally). And now it begins.

The wait.

Just wait until that professor gets something wrong, just wait. He will eventually—absolutely none of Noah's teachers live and breathe to be right the way he does.

Mispronounce something, please.

Mix up the year it happened, please.

Put a concept so simply that you're all but begging Noah to say, "Well, actually," please.

Even just one score a week could sustain Noah happily, but it would be so beautiful to set the tone of the year right, right off the bat.

Noah's at the top of the room, in one of the back seats of this amphitheater-looking lecture hall, sitting straight up (no slouching soporific in his seat like his classmates), and gazing down over this sea of his so-called peers. The professor is droning on about attendance policies and the school's code of conduct, reading off a prepared statement, when all together the students shift slightly.

Small lights are zooming across the ceiling, reflected and whirling off a pair of army dog tags being spun on a chain by some skinhead-looking kid in the third row. The dude is an absolute child, sneering and bored, with all the attitude Noah himself has, but with much less justification. He's too young to have earned those tags in service, for example, and even if they're a family member's and not just some mass-stamped jewelry from the mall, Noah hates him for the way he's twirling them on that necklace, letting lights and motion entertain him like some bouncer-bound brat, even as it distracts everyone else who might be here to learn, or at least listen.

Noah fantasizes about being in the seat behind that boy as the teacher continues the same spiel Noah heard when he first attended this school at fourteen. He imagines what it would feel like to reach forward and snatch that chain back onto the kid's throat, twisting and pulling it tight like a garrote.

The kid stops his little game a moment before the professor looks up, the luck of the loutish saving him from a reprimand.

The class is a waste of time. Here's your syllabus, let's go through each point aloud as if no one here can read. Everybody say a little about yourself, name and major and why you're taking this class (like it matters). Well, now there isn't enough time left to do justice to a lecture so go home and read the first assignment in the textbook. Noah is frowning as he leaves the classroom, grumbling to himself, "That's a chunk of my life I'll never get back again," when he is overheard by a passing professor, a man so old and established at this campus that he's all but morphing into an emeritus with each lapsing second.

The man frowns at Noah, offended on behalf of his colleague, until he rears back and peeks through the door. When he sees the man who just wasted Noah's precious time, he grimaces.

"We're not supposed to speak ill of our fellow faculty, but . . . hmm. Put it this way: his *wife* is an excellent asset to the science department."

Noah snorts, and then remembers exactly who this man is, and then says, "Professor Rudell, I don't know if you remember me, but I just transferred back and I was wondering—"

"You're Kaplan, the one with the articles on . . . bugs?"

"Birds."

"Even better." Professor Rudell beckons Noah to walk with him, his arm reaching out from his jacket sleeve and revealing the fish-belly flesh of his wrist. He pincers Noah's shoulder with his craggy fingers. "I've been wanting an underclassman to help me organize material for my TAs. I need someone who knows how to write and knows what a deadline is, but I don't like bugs. Are you free on Wednesdays?"

"Totally free," Noah says, pleased with Professor Rudell for reading his mind like this. Noah promised his mother, almost the last thing he said to her before she died, that he would have a stellar college career, but he never got around to it in Michigan, not with Ray eclipsing everything.

"Come to my next office hours and we'll set it up," Rudell says, releasing Noah from his grip and pointing at him. "Glad to see you've returned, young man."

Noah is nearly smiling as he exits the corridor into the outer hallway. He is thinking of how his mother would approve, of how his whole family will think better of him now after the waffling he did in trying to follow Ray to U of M, and in this pleasant haze of having his reputation precede him, Noah finds himself in front of a bulletin board advertising school clubs.

There's one for a Latin Club, for a Spanish Table, for an Italian Society. Noah's got an aptitude for language, one that crosses into his ability to correctly identify and locate birdcalls. He's been meaning to research the connection at some point but . . . perhaps it can wait until after he joins a few clubs, maybe makes a few friends, maybe discusses the topic with one of them first.

Noah jots down the contact info for every language club he can see, and scratches down a reminder about his appointment with Professor Rudell, and all the while he's shaking his head at himself: how had he forgotten that Ray wasn't the only smart person on the planet? Noah resolves that his whole life will improve from today onward, now that he's out of Ray's charming aura, and finally free.

10

SCORCHED EARTH, THAT'S HOW RAY thinks of this past semester without Noah. The mercury's high, the ashes glow red, and will continue to smolder for hours and days and weeks to come. This semester is Chernobyl. This semester is the Hiroshima bomb, it's a mushroom cloud that billows so thick it almost looks comfortable.

He drank too much this year. Tanked, that's the word for it. He tanked because he was tanked. He didn't totally fail, but he disappointed everyone. A C-average student. An average student. A let-down.

Now Ray's sitting in front of a counselor. A counselor with babyish curls in his hair, and a cozy turtleneck sweater on, and the kind eyes of a mother above a full and robust beard.

"You came into this school with a lot of potential, Raymond."

"Call me Ray," he says. X-Ray, death Ray, a Ray of nuclear light.

"Do you feel like you've lived up to that potential, Ray?"

"Of course I haven't, but it doesn't matter. Grades don't matter in college."

"Well, yes they do," the counselor says. Ray bets himself that this is the huggy counselor, the one they send you to if they think you might cry. Ray doesn't cry. He hasn't cried in at least ten years.

"You know," Ray says, reaching out to spike the drinky bird on this guy's desk so he'll have something interesting to take his attention, "most people think these things are perpetual motion machines, but it's actually a heat engine." That's something Noah told him when they saw one in the school store the first day they arrived in Michigan and had gone out together to explore the campus. Ray often quotes Noah when he wants to feel smart.

"Really? How? It's not warm."

"I don't know," Ray says, watching the bird (who has no water to drink, the poor bastard) try to pound its head on the desk and always just miss it. "Ask someone who gets better grades."

The counselor smiles understandingly at him. "This session isn't about criticizing you, Ray. We recognize that college has a lot of challenges that have nothing to do with how smart you are. Time management, a social life, love, sex, friendship, money, all kinds of adult things are hitting you all at once, and you being so much younger than most of your classmates, you've actually done really well. You certainly haven't failed anything, you haven't gotten into any trouble, you joined a fraternity, which is excellent, that'll give you plenty of stability and support going forward next year. Some of your professors just recommended that I touch base with you, make sure you know I'm here. If you ever feel overwhelmed, you can come talk to me and we'll work it out."

"Which of my professors thought I needed counseling? Was it Beekman? I bet it was her, she really didn't like me."

"This isn't punitive, Ray," Mr. Sensitive reiterates, and then seems to decide to go the extra mile. "You know, you remind me a lot of myself at your age," he says. "I held myself to pretty high standards and it caused me to have a rough year once too, but look: I'm living proof that you can recover from this and still have a great life."

Ray clamps both lips in between his teeth and looks out the window at the building's generators to compose this in a way that won't get him expelled.

"Um, no offense, but if this—" Ray waves his hand to encompass the whole office with its dusty blinds and neutral walls and the fucking drinky bird on the desk that's just begging to get its pipey neck snapped "—is all I have to look forward to, I'd rather be hanged."

The counselor makes a tsk noise and grimaces.

"I hope you're not thinking of harming yourself, Raymond, and if you're just being flip, this isn't really the appropriate time or place."

"It was just a figure of speech," Ray says, changing his demeanor to the one he knows everyone likes, the one that gets them off his back no matter what the problem is. "I was only joking." Smile, cock the head downward and subservient-like, shrug of one shoulder.

"It's not a very funny joke, but your professors did say you like to make your classmates laugh." He takes a card off his desk and hands it to Ray, with his name that Ray still doesn't bother to know, and his contact information in case Ray wants to flush some more of his life away.

"Alright, thanks, you know," Ray says, standing up and lunging for the door. "This has made me feel sort of better, so thanks."

He's in the hallway, he slams into the press-bar of the side door, he can't leave fast enough.

He will have to get his grades up, he knows that. He's already got his ZBT brothers grumbling about his drinking, he doesn't need them on his case about his grade average too. He can't get kicked out of the house, he can't get kicked out of school, and he certainly can't become one of those idiots who somehow manages to sabotage themselves just before the finish line.

And good lord . . . just imagine what Noah would think of him! Noah who went back to Chicago and spent all semester proving himself: perfect grades, a TA-ship or something, and he's even talking to girls in French and Italian (hopefully about something other than himself—people do get sick of hearing about how smart he is), taking them out bird-watching, becoming everybody's perfect gentlemen.

Ray doesn't want to begrudge Noah his successes, and in a way Ray regards them as his own victories as well; Noah's newfound graces are clearly the result of his attendance at the Raymond Klein Finishing School, but . . . it's horrible to think that such an unpromising student has surpassed such a once-sterling master.

Everyone in Ray's life will be let down if he keeps screwing up like this, but nobody has ever thought more highly of him than Noah, and a fall that far could shatter a boy so used to being admired.

LIKELY
SONS

1

THE DAY NOAH F. KAPLAN, Jr. was born, everyone knew he was the family's last baby. That made him *the* baby. Not just the most recent baby, but the baby boy, the baby brother, for the rest of his life.

He was the third son, but very nearly the fifth miscarriage. His oldest brother was born with very few problems, but Michael was followed by two miscarriages, Samuel put his mother in bed for six months just to be born, then two more miscarriages in the pursuit of a daughter, and then Noah: a full pregnancy immobile, and it left his mother's kidneys in irrevocable distress. Bad kidneys ran in the generations above her, and they'd probably appear in her children as well, is what everyone thought but didn't say.

With Mother so ill and her first two boys so young and boisterous, nurses were employed. There was a household to run, a good old-fashioned household with a cook and a maid and a man for the yard; a machine, oiled by father's elbow grease and fan-belted with money.

The baby was sick too. Born just a touch too soon, underweight and with fussy lungs. Since neither one was contagious, mother and baby were held aloft together from the rest of the family like crazy coots, up on the second floor, in a room with plenty of light and airy windows, a room where a healthy woman might love to paint.

And that year, of course, winter came early, and boxed mother Faye into her own personal Overlook Hotel. And the light hardly ever warmed from the corpse-like blue-white light that glows out of snow. And the slush running in the streets made the help unreliable. And sunlamps couldn't touch the seasonal depression, which compounded with her post-partum doldrums in ways that quietly floored her; the combination was simply, stunningly stupefying. And the baby was her only real company, as Mike and Sam romped shamelessly outside her windows, and Noah Sr. went to work and went to work and went to work.

She might have resented the baby's presence if Noah Jr. had been like her other sons were as infants. Any discomfort experienced by those boys and they'd scream the roof to the ground, but not Noah. He would only grunt and squirm in frustration, like he knew what he wanted to do, but his fine motor skills just hadn't developed yet! It endeared him to his mother, the way he laid there like a lump and fumed noiselessly when something was wrong. It was as if he didn't want to bother her, but damned if he could figure out how to change his own diaper, so Faye helped him out.

"Good morning, sweet baby," she began greeting him each day, and each day she started to mean it more and more truly. "Good morning and happy day, my sweet baby, let's wake up!"

More often than not the baby seemed to roll his eyes at her, but that only spurred their conversations into healthy debates.

"I know you feel that way now, and in all honesty so do I," Faye told him, "but you won't remember these first few months someday, nobody ever does." Faye had the strength some mornings to get on a pair of thick socks and her fleece sweater and push the bassinet over to the window where she had a heavily-cushioned rocking chair she liked to ease into. "Hopefully we timed it right so that your first memory will be of spring, my love. Maybe Mommy will feel better by then too, wouldn't that be nice? And maybe someday, somehow you'll remember us both stepping out into sunshine for the first time. My hair has a little bit of red in it, but you can't see that in this light. And who knows what you're like in the sun, hmm? Maybe you're secretly happy. Maybe you'll get some of your granny's freckles, or turn auburn like your one cousin, what do you think?"

Noah frowned and blew a burble with his lips. Most of his noises were like those that came out of small, shook up jugs of liquid.

"*So* moody, aren't you? Or maybe you're just gassy, hmm? Which end did that noise come out of, hmm? Well, Mommy's gassy too, and it's all your fault, but I don't blame you. It's not like you meant to tie a bunch of knots in here, is it?" Faye patted her torso gently, the same way she did when it was occupied, smoothing her nightgown with fingers that had aged drastically over this last pregnancy, that looked more like her mother's fingers than her own, all knobby knuckles and deep lines. Normally she preferred to sleep in pajama pants, but the waistband was too tight for her now, squeezing her kidneys uncomfortably. She imagined her insides all stirred up and tender like a chunky stew and hoped this baby of all of the three would be the most worth it, hoped he would end up being her favorite in the years to come.

"I do hope you're worth all this trouble," she told him.

Baby Noah continued to make more bubbling noises, but also did a double leg-stomp for emphasis on whatever he was trying to communicate.

"No, no, baby, no promises yet, just know we expect great things from you, okay? Straight A's, a good job, a heap of grandchildren, but take your time, take your time." The snow outside turned to ice and started to sting the glass of the window. "You've got plenty of time."

2

WHEN RAYMOND A. KLEIN WAS brought home from the hospital, it was about six months and two blocks away, a season and a world away.

The month was peachy June, and he was in the arms of a woman who bloomed with motherhood, who was herself born for it. This was her third son too, just like Faye, but Anna Klein was flush, plump, sturdy, and knew she wanted at least one more, maybe two (maybe twins!), before she put up her maternity pants for good. Her pregnancies were fortifying up until those last few heavy, uncomfortable months: thick hair, full bosom, clear complexion. Nausea, yes, always, but the kind of nausea that is charmingly cured by applying sweetened fruit. Candied pineapples, sugared strawberries, syrupy salads of bright coastal oranges or pastel balls of melons, slices of apples that had recently hung like Christmas ornaments in the halls of some Southern orchard. Anna was all natural, a natural; she made having babies look easy.

Two days home from the hospital and she was restless enough for a walk around the block. Babies are certainly cute but they're *dreadful* company. Anna usually kept the TV on for company and hopefully for verbal education, because her babies got no goo-goo talk from her. She felt like a fool when she tried, the way she felt trying to interact with a pet. But the TV wasn't enough that day either.

On a day that called for rain but was holding sunny all afternoon, with her older two boys playing some headless chicken run-around game under the harried watch of their nanny, Anna put baby Raymond in the same old family stroller and took him outside. She waved hi to a few people who were out on their lawns either cussing quietly at their lawn mowers or just getting the mail, but no one who gave her the impression they'd stand still for a conversation.

It wasn't until she got two blocks down her street and decided to hang a righty to head back home, that she finally spotted Mrs. Rosen out misting her perennials against the so-far rainless day.

A rainbow trembled in the spray from Mrs. Rosen's hose. The hose was like a ghost detector, Anna's socially starved brain thought; maybe there were rainbows all around, all the time, and a bright mist of water only revealed them.

Mrs. Rosen finally noticed Anna's frantic approach, and with a reluctant face turned to speak to her, as if she realized she couldn't very well throw down the hose and sprint inside now that she'd been spotted.

"How's that baby?" Mrs. Rosen said, looking down at Ray and leaning over to put his binky back in his mouth (Anna hadn't noticed that he'd pushed it out and was airing his chubby little tongue around the neighborhood). "And how many does this make again?"

Anna laughed, so relieved to at last be talking to a grown-up. "Number three, another boy! They do seem to be piling up, don't they?"

Mrs. Rosen nodded slowly, and rubbed a hand across the back of her neck in a masculine gesture. Even then Mrs. Rosen had the short, spiky, iron-colored hair of a woman who'd given up on skirts forever.

"And how is Mr. Klein, happy to have another son? Some men really dislike having too few sons, you know, no matter what they say." Mrs. Rosen was in her fifties, with three grown-ish daughters and no sons of her own, and everyone knew her husband was having at least one affair. It was making her bitter.

"Oh, busy, you know." Mr. Klein was second in command behind the CEO of Sears, but his wife knew better than to be ostentatious about his high position. She touched back some of her own long hair, promising herself that she'd never let it be too inconvenient to keep beautiful. "The other morning at breakfast he was a million miles away, stirring his spoon in his coffee like he was ringing a bell, it was driving me crazy! And no matter how many times I said 'hon, *hon*' he never looked up. I finally stuck my head in the freezer trying to muffle the sound."

Mrs. Rosen smiled tightly and started rolling up her hose. "Better the freezer than the oven, dear."

Anna wanted to beg her to stay, to keep talking with her please, but only said, "Done watering?"

"No need anymore, here comes that rain."

Anna turned to where Mrs. Rosen had indicated, over her shoulder like someone might have just walked up behind them to interrupt. The sky was roiling towards them, bubbling up as thick and black as oil out of the ground.

"Oh, shoot, I better run."

"Want an umbrella?" Mrs. Rosen offered, but Anna was already back on the street, already out of breath enough to have to wave a wordless thanks behind her.

Anna returned to her own street just as the first few drops of rain started hitting the baby. She didn't coo any comfort to him, just got them both safely inside before it started really coming down. In the time it took her to fold up the stroller and get back into the living room, the whole daylight had changed. Her living room, bright when she left it, now had a very dramatic solar eclipse sort of light.

She popped the baby back into his bouncy chair and circled the living room opening up windows, really putting her shoulder into the task. She wanted to let the noise and the smell of the storm in, listen to the applause of the drops as they flickered around the house, hitting leaves and concrete, drumming the roof.

Anna got nearly thirty seconds of this exhilarating peace before baby Ray took a deep breath and started to howl.

Anna sighed as the nanny came downstairs, a young lady they'd lured out of a local day care center and into private service with better money.

"He's got a set of pipes on him, doesn't he? I just put Eric down for his nap and Allen's in the play room with a movie."

"Well, see if you can't do something with this one, he just started with this, probably tired."

Anna slid the bouncer away from her, and went to close up the windows, since water was starting to spray in through the screens.

"Babies usually sleep to the sound of rain, maybe I can get him to settle down."

"You do that," Anna said, staring out at the sopping-wet afternoon. Anna knew that was the last bit of adult conversation she'd have all day.

She closed the curtains on the windows.

3

WHEN NOAH WAS FOUR YEARS old, he drew a furious bird's nest in crayon that hung on the fridge for nearly two years (and now resides in a file box in the basement labeled NOAH with every report card he's ever brought home). He had already completed a brief sketch of a house, an impression of a doggy, and a portrait of Mommy. Mommy looked disturbingly unlike herself and more like Noah's German au pair, Nadine—mostly because of the blond hair. The real Mommy had very dark hair, but the real Mommy also had a torso, not just legs sticking out of her head, so . . . maybe it wasn't that big a deal.

His current drawing was a very serious rendering of a robin's nest, not that Noah knew it at the time. With blue circles for eggs already set down, a chaotic brown scribbling was being thatched in for the twigs of the nest. Nadine bustled around the kitchen table as he did this work, stirring up a pitcher of iced tea and constructing a meal for Noah—folding a sandwich together, washing cherry tomatoes, cutting up a hot dog into a pot of macaroni and cheese, most of which would be put into the fridge and served to him for tomorrow and the next day's lunches as well. She watched Noah work in between doing her own, squinting.

"Tongue is out again," Nadine told him, touching Noah's peeking tongue with a thick, salty finger. "I see it again another time, I slap it back in. You look like stupid animal otherwise."

Noah tucked his tongue back behind his teeth, hating the taste of it now, kind of wanting to suck on one of his crayons, but that would get him a pop on the face for sure. Nadine sat down, stared steadily at Noah, and crossed her arms over her substantial bosom. She tucked one hand into her armpit and rested the other one on the opposite elbow, leaving it poised to strike out should Noah's tongue reappear. He locked his teeth together as he returned to drawing. The muscles in his cheeks quivered and tightened under his springy young skin.

The stand-off was broken when Mike came through the kitchen—newly bar mitzvahed, taller than he was just a few weeks before, with a deep voice that tuned in occasionally for longer and longer stretches. To Noah, Mike was exactly as old as he had always been before, but Nadine took pains to compliment Mike on his new adulthood whenever they crossed paths.

"Ah, here is the handsome man!" The hand that Nadine had prepped for smacking Noah was being used to grasp Mike's arm, and Noah relaxed back into his work. She would bother Mike for a while now.

"Yeah, hey," Mike said. His arms were bare, he was in his workout shirt with the sleeves cut off so he could admire his developing muscles, but this meant that Nadine could admire them too.

"Noah, you want to be handsome like your brother someday?" she asked.

"Nein," Noah said, answering back in Nadine's native tongue. He could already converse as naturally in German as he could in English, and he sometimes considered German easier. He knew the rest of his family couldn't understand him in German, and so when Nadine wasn't around, he could speak aloud and still keep his thoughts private. He liked the feeling of being inscrutable.

"What was that, was that 'no'?" Mike snorted. "No worries there, baby brother, you look like a frog. Trust me, you'll have to be rich to get married."

"He is just a child, he says many of strange things," Nadine assured Mike. "He loves his big brother." She pinched Noah's ear, a little too hard, but he knows why. She just liked Mike so much, everybody did, everybody but Mommy, who seemed to like anyone who would spend time with her, which Noah did. A lot of time, in fact. Mommy told him about birds, about all the prettiest birds, and Mommy was who this picture was for, that was why he concentrated so hard on it. It was important not to let the nest scribble over the eggs, not to mess up how perfectly Noah believed he had gotten those small blue circles. He had almost managed to get it perfect too, when Nadine's hand clapped onto his face.

"Tongue," she said, "so disgusting."

Mike laughed, got the glass of water he must have come in for, and walked out again. Nadine put down Noah's dinner, moved the picture aside as she did so. The smack had made Noah flinch. One of the eggs had a big brown scrawl right through it, ruining the whole thing.

Noah ate his dinner quickly, could taste nothing in his mouth except the salt of Nadine's palm and the form and shape of his food.

When done, Noah said with as much authority he could muster, "I'm taking my picture to Mommy."

Nadine excused him with a wave. He could hear her murmuring in German he didn't know yet, a sound that mingled with the tap and clack of dishes in the sink. She was cleaning up before she went home. Noah ascended the stairs to find his mother.

It was impossible to know if she was sleeping from the doorway of her room. She was always in bed, always breathing deeply and seemingly restful. Sometimes she had a book over there, some headphones plugged in, and sometimes she was sleeping, any time of the day or night, it didn't matter.

Noah walked in quietly with the picture held facing him. She opened her eyes when he approached, and smiled.

"I made you this." Noah handed over the picture, irritated but trying not to show it in front of her. "This part was an accident, but I made it for you."

"Thank you, I love it." She looked more at him than at the picture as she said this. She patted the bed beside her. "Hop up."

Noah did. Mommy's bed always had sort of a sour-sweet smell, like a not-quite-gone-over cantaloupe, but Noah didn't mind. He crawled over her so he could curl up in the space closest to the wall, but was careful not to put any of his weight on Mommy's body.

Like robin's eggs, Mommy was delicate.

4

WHEN RAY WAS FOUR YEARS AND eleven months old, he was taken to his first baseball game at Wrigley Field. It was meant to be a present for his fifth birthday, since he was 'practically five' according to Dad. He became practically a lot of things after that.

"I'm practically asleep," he would say when his nanny asked him why he wasn't in bed yet.

"I'm practically done," he would assure when someone pointed out at dinner that he hadn't touched his vegetables.

"I'm practically grown up!" he would shout when the real grown-ups saw through this ploy, and forced their will on him anyway.

Ray's Uncle Sid took him to his first Cubs game, after his father got them both tickets. It was a scheduling nightmare to clear a whole day just to treat one kid, so birthday treats happened whenever they were most convenient, with whomever was available at the time.

The cratered space of the stadium was the biggest thing Ray had ever seen, the diamond-patterned grass of the field reminded him of a snake, and the sun and air seemed different up in the seats than it did on the streets, seemed freer. Ray envied that.

Ray was five years and one month old the second time he went to a baseball game, and by this time he had learned how to lie. No more practically anything, things either were or weren't, according to Ray's word. In the past few weeks his teeth had gone unbrushed, his bed unmade, his vitamins hidden in his mouth to be flushed away later, unswallowed. All his life he had been so beholden to the truth, angered by it, insistent on it, but it turned out lying was so much faster and easier, and no one yet suspected him.

Getting into the car after the second game, Uncle Sid asked Ray which game he had liked better.

Ray said, "I've only been to one." It wasn't a lie that could get him anything he wanted, as far as he knew, but it was always good to practice. In fact, just then he was in the back seat, only holding his seatbelt across his body, not fastening it. He could get away with *anything*, if he wanted to.

"You don't remember coming here before?" Uncle Sid asked. Ray thought for a moment he was turning around to look at Ray in total disbelief, but he was only backing out.

"No," Ray told his Uncle Sid's jowly face.

"You don't remember how we could see into the dugout, or that big hot dog with the sparklers on it? You don't remember those sparklers?"

"No." Ray absolutely remembered those sparklers. He was disappointed that they hadn't made a reappearance this time, but last time was a special occasion, and today was just an occasion. He hadn't gotten a baseball cupcake with a candle sticking out of it either, come to think of it. This game was definitely less exciting than the last.

"Well, that's too bad," said Uncle Sid. "It would have been a really nice memory."

It became a topic of conversation that night at dinner, the question of when kids formed their first lifelong memory. Among the adults it was asked: what was everyone's oldest memory?

"I was four or five," Mother said, touching her hair and neck excessively, the way she did whenever she drank out of the tulip glasses that were for grown-ups only. "I tried to run away through my window and I pushed the screen out? Then I just sat down and cried in the mirror thinking I had broken it and that my mother was going to hate me. My father came around and snapped it back in without telling her though. Or maybe he did tell her, I guess it wasn't as big a catastrophe as I thought it was then."

"I remember stealing a toy race car from some kid in the first grade," said Dad. "Who was that weird kid who always wore the shirt with Saturn on it?"

"You mean the kid who later beat you for valedictorian, Al?" Sid said. "Yeah, I'm really sure you forgot his name."

The adults all laughed, and Dad made his hand into the symbol Ray's brothers told him meant bird. Ray made his own bird, with much difficulty, in solidarity and salute. This got his brothers laughing too, and Mother swatted at Dad as she cupped her other hand around Ray's and told him, "That's not a nice thing to do."

Sid started telling his own story about a youthful bike crash that gave him his one crooked tooth, and Ray sat in the midst of all this commotion, ecstatic.

Dinnertime was always *so boring*, usually involving conversation about news or business, or what the older boys did at school, but this? Laughter, volume, *focus* on Ray the likes of which he usually only got when he was in trouble . . . this was awesome.

This would be his first memory.

5

WHEN NOAH WAS SIX YEARS old, he was enrolled in Our Lady of the Snowfall, an all-girls Catholic school nine blocks from his family's home. Well, there was one other boy in attendance, but he was older, and he and Noah didn't associate. It was a circumstance that had come about in a lot of little ways.

Noah's au pair had run him through every pre-school test there was, had taught him concepts up to second grade comprehension before he was old enough for kindergarten, and it was time—she insisted—that he start getting real schooling so he wouldn't lose the advantage he had because of all her hard work. Everyone was agreeable to the idea of starting the boy in school, even Noah, but his mother didn't want him going too far away. She didn't want him crossing streets or taking buses, she didn't want so much of their time together to be eaten away by meaningless travel. School was good for him, but lengthy transport? She desired that be kept to a minimum. Noah's father insisted on the best school they could find: highest test scores, newest facilities, best college placement years down the line for the kids. Only one school met all of their requirements.

Sure, Snowfall was all girls, but it was in the process of (very slowly) integrating boys. It was Catholic in foundation and insisted on school-wide moments of prayer three times a day, but religious classes were not mandatory if the family chose to opt out. It cost quite a bit of money, but so it should! There were nutritionists in the cafeteria, former Chicago police guarding the grounds, and PhDs throughout the faculty. Snowfall was proposed, considered, accepted. At six years old Noah started second grade classes, and thus began the most peaceful period of his life.

Were the girls mean? Yes, sometimes, but mostly to each other.

Were their questions very intrusive? Yes, but they did value honesty.

Was Noah in high demand during recess? Absolutely, he was (for once in his life) incredibly popular.

"We're playing princesses! You have to be the king," screamed the bossiest girl, Jessica, on the very first day. "Here's your crown." The crown was two spiky, branching twigs tucked behind his ears. "This is your cape." She tied the sleeves of someone's red jacket over his shoulders. "Go to the top of the jungle gym and you judge the princess contest for who gets to marry the prince, okay?"

Noah stood on the top platform of the metal play structure, gripped the safety rail's smooth candy-colored coating, and looked out over what felt to him like acres of a wood-chip carpeted kingdom, voting up or down with his thumbs. The power of it, the towering height, the way the girls all listened to him even if they didn't like what he decided, because he was special. It was clear to him right there and then that being special was the best way to be.

But of course, heavy is the head that wears the crown. He witnessed tantrums the likes of which he had never thrown himself—hysterical, drenched in real tears. He had to suffer the indignity of being demoted from king to prince for the wedding ceremony to Jessica (he had picked her because he knew her best, and because she seemed like precisely the wrong person to slight). Jessica pulled three tissues from a pack in her lunch box and fixed them around her head with a polka-dotted headband for her veil. The favored girls in her hen clutch became bridesmaids and her frenemies became groomsmen (if they didn't stop playing entirely). Noah had to hold hands and recite vows for the rest of recess, but it wasn't so bad. At least he wasn't being made fun of, or ignored, or stripped and examined as his brothers had told him might happen.

"You know girls don't have anything down there," Mike told him in the weeks approaching his first day.

"It's flat and smooth," confirmed Sam, "just take the clothes off one of their dolls sometime, we're not making this stuff up."

"They're going to want to see your Thing," they assured him.

Mike nodded sagely as they had the last of these talks the night before Noah's first day. "It's just a natural curiosity, but like, they're not going to ask, they're just going to tackle you at some point, probably."

"And you know, one by one they're not that strong," Sam added, "but they're all going to be older than you, and there will be *a lot* of them where you're going."

"Yep, you're going to be on their turf, Noah, so just . . . be prepared."

Both boys patted him fraternally on the shoulder before walking out of his room and bursting into laughter. For all their warnings, Noah guessed they thought it was pretty funny that he was about to be humiliated and exposed.

But no one wanted to look at his Thing; its secret presence did cause the girls to treat him differently than they treated each other, but the Thing never had to be verified or even spoken of, much to Noah's relief. It didn't occur to him until well after he got home that his brothers had been lying to him. And he didn't think to ask for the real facts until weeks into the school year, walking home with Nadine on a mid-week day.

"Do girls have Things?" he asked her abruptly, so abruptly that she hissed between her teeth before answering him, an indication of her displeasure. He had also pointed at his own crotch, so she wouldn't misunderstand him.

"No," she said.

"They really are flat down there? Like dolls?" He had investigated some of the dolls in the play area at school—sure enough, be they made of cloth or plastic, every one had nothing but a smooth plane of nothing.

"Not flat. Girls have two holes like you only have one. Your brothers know that for sure."

"Oh. I *thought* they were lying," Noah told Nadine, hoping she wouldn't think he was stupid.

"*Schweine*," she mumbled as she patted Noah's head kindly. "They lie but you don't. You're a good boy."

Noah nodded. Good, yes, and possibly the best. Being the only boy those first few years made it very hard not to be the best one. It gave him a taste for it.

6

When Ray was nine years old, he became an older brother. His next older brother, Eric, was starting high school. The brother above that, Allen, was about to graduate high school. Enter Tommy: squalling, pink, hot, heavy, awful, and he wouldn't be interesting enough for Ray to interact with for years. It was like someone sank a bowling ball into a bathtub full of warm, resting water; he displaced everything in Ray's perfect life.

Ray's playroom? It became a nursery once more, and Ray was encouraged to play outside. The babying he was used to? Robbed from him, he was expected to behave significantly better than ever before. Ray's nanny became Tommy's nanny, and Ray? He got a tutor instead.

"Who is she?" he demanded of his mother when an interviewing visit was announced.

"Keep your voice down," his mother told him with the quiet, foreboding voice she used only in malls, grocery stores, and grandma's house—it was the you-will-not-embarrass-Mommy-in-front-of-other-adults voice. Ray despised this voice. It meant his mother was completely immune to all his tricks and charms.

"I don't want her! I don't need a tutor!"

"Hey, the baby is sleeping, can you get him under control?" Ray's father asked. He was here to meet the tutor lady, Tracy, and make sure she fit in well with their family goals. He kept checking his watch, adjusting his tie; he had somewhere to be very soon. 'Family goals' was Ray's mother's phrase. Ray's father didn't believe he was required for this particular chore. He was impatient. Mother was irritated. Ray was inflamed with injustice.

"I don't like her!"

"You haven't even met her yet," Father said, sitting down just as the doorbell rang, on one of the chairs no one ever used because they faced nothing but the front door.

Ray's mother took a firm but even clamp on Ray's upper arm, the kind of hold that hurt but wouldn't leave bruises, and brought him with her towards the door.

Ray twisted his own arm violently, an animal in a trap that must lose a limb or be clubbed to death by an approaching hunter. His mother's face came close to his, her mouth opened to scold him, but she hesitated for a moment at his unreasonable ferocity, and in that hesitation Ray was able to escape.

Ray dangled all his weight off his arm, which forced his mother to lower him to the ground lest he twist it right off, and let him go.

Ray shot up off the ground as everyone moved into place around him, his mother to the door with a soul-shaking sigh, his father to the balls of his feet, robotically happy when greeting another employee. Ray's well-behaved brothers, including baby Tommy in the arms of a woman Ray now considered a traitor, filed down the stairs as Ray himself rushed up, and into his former playroom.

He delivered a smack to his rocking horse for being there, vigilant, but never moving to help. He snatched his telescope from its stand by the sunny window, returned to the ground, and army-crawled back into the hallway. He could hear his parents apologizing to this tutor, this *Tracy*, before he was close enough to see through the banister. He poked the telescope out through the slats to get a good look at this new lady. He needed to get the measure of her before she got the jump on him.

Ray first got this telescope a year before. He used it like a theater prop for the first two months he had it, half the time not even looking through the lens when he held it up to his eye, playing detective or pirate or sniper. It came with a tripod and was probably meant to stay installed and stationary, but Ray preferred to take it with him bike-riding and tree-climbing. He carried it around like a baton.

When Ray finally realized its intended purpose, it was like he'd invented it all on his own. It's just that he hadn't seen anything interesting enough in the real world to want a good look at it—didn't know how to hunt or stalk yet, didn't know how to spy—until this stranger walked into his house, looking for him.

"Raymond is being a brat right now," his mother said to a tall woman with glasses on a chain around her neck and a large backpack that looked wildly out of place on an adult. "These are our other boys."

Ray watched them shake hands, coo at the baby some, and start talking child-rearing as the grown men fled in three separate directions.

Eric came up the stairs and swatted Ray on the head when he spotted him in his crow's nest at the top of the steps, messing up the boy's neatly parted hair.

"Mom's gonna kill you if you don't go down there soon," he said. "Take your homework with you if you want to avoid punishment, you're supposed to start with her today."

"I don't want to!"

Eric snorted at him, and before shutting himself back into his room, told Ray, "That didn't save me and Allen and it sure as hell won't help you. Now go study."

Ray took in an outraged breath, one that reached all the way to the floor, where his knees were getting carpet burn. He knew his brother was right; the longer he left his mother making excuses for him, the sorrier he would be.

Defeated and bitter, he let fall his telescope and got his school folders from his room. The trudge downstairs was as grim a march as he had ever taken. He walked into the dining room just as he heard Tracy saying, "It's never too early to prepare for college," and looked her square in the eye.

"There's our young man," Tracy said with a nod. He nodded back at her. "Sit down, we have a lot of work to do."

7

When Noah was eleven years old, the number three woman in his life got fired.

It was a given variable that Nadine would have to leave eventually, because of course Noah would grow up and no longer need anyone governing him day to day. His brothers had sloughed off their care-takers by the time they entered middle school, so once the summer of his eleventh year was upon Noah, he expected Nadine to move on. To another kid, maybe, or to another city, or maybe go home to Germany where her sister still lived, maybe get married. She was in her thirties by this time, and she talked often to Noah about her married friends, the age stats of her peer group, women who had gotten married at nineteen, at twenty-three, at twenty-six . . . at some point already. "I am around suited young men all day," she would say about Noah and his brothers, snatching at their cheeks for a pinch, "but I am never married."

With maturity fast approaching, and a probable growth spurt in the works, it was time to trade out Noah's old kiddie twin bed for a full-sized one. The small one Nadine took apart on her own, so that the delivery men would have room to set up the new one. Noah tried to help her at first, but it was a frustrating, finger-pinching task, and she snapped at him, "Leave me to be!" Her command was punctuated by the clang of a dropped wrench.

Noah and Nadine were in a wary state around this bed. That swap—the old for the new—externalized their situation too plainly. All spring Dad had been talking to his friends about what to give Nadine as a severance bonus, trying to feel around for a fair number. Aunt Clarice, on Mom's behalf, kept suggesting next steps for her, other families she knew with young children. Or something fun, perhaps? Vacation! Travel! Maybe she could go into business for herself, huh? It was leading inexorably to one final thing: Nadine's dismissal.

Noah bounced happily onto his new bed, a fresh comforter thrown over it to give him an idea of the change it made in the room. Navy and gray stripes, the heavy, shiny wooden bedposts at all four corners—it looked so grown up, so distinguished. He loved it.

"Up!" Nadine snapped at him after Dad and Aunt Clarice left the doorway. Dad had congratulated Noah on growing up so fast (not really a personal accomplishment of Noah's, but still praise, and still appreciated), and Aunt Clarice took a couple of pictures to show her sister, who didn't think she could handle the stairs today to see the room herself. There was talk of installing a stair lift for Faye, a seat that could motor her up and down with all the speed and mobility of the elderly or paraplegic, but she insisted on getting along without it—said she'd be a literal Lazy Susan and refused.

"The bed is not made yet," Nadine told Noah louder, since he didn't listen to her the first time. "Hurry, get up!"

Noah was fluffing around over the plush new spread like a dust-bathing sparrow—flapping left, then right, then clutching the blanket so he became a burrito. When he was fully encased like this, wrapped up and defenseless, Nadine lost her patience entirely, grabbed him by the ankles, and yanked.

Noah came crashing bodily to the floor, the breath knocked all the way out of him, his back in a seizure of spasmodic horror. He'd landed right on his coccyx, and for a moment he felt no pain, and for a few more moments he could not speak of the pain.

"Oh, thanks very much for letting me do my work," Nadine said sarcastically, stepping over him while unfurling a fitted sheet. It wasn't until a whistling teapot sort of wail started to leak from Noah that Nadine turned to look at him, and in turning, she finally noticed who else had made it into the room.

Noah's mother, arms akimbo, hands in the small of her back, must have decided this was too big a milestone to miss because of a few steps. She held Nadine in a furious glare as Noah started to worm his way towards her, but Faye could do nothing to comfort him, not even bend down closer to wipe the tears that had started oozing up into his eyes.

"Help him up," Faye ordered, and Nadine did, her expression lemon-sucked and resigned.

Returned to the bed, Noah gently tried to straighten out his back, but lying flat was no good. He curled onto his side, fetal and helpless.

"I think you should gather up your things and go," Faye said. "Mr. Kaplan will call you later with a decision about what's to be done."

Nadine stood affronted for a beat, then rolled her eyes and departed. It was an inauspicious end to nearly a decade of service, and a lifetime of rearing for Noah. His mother was quick to make that relationship seem insignificant.

"I'll get Aunt Clarice to get you some aspirin and my other heating pad, hmm? I'll take care of you," Faye said, sitting down and rubbing her son's back. "You're too old for nannies now anyway, so I expect that's the last we'll have of Miss Nadine."

Noah squirmed his head onto her lap and closed his eyes. "Okay," he said. The muscles along his lower back felt screaming hot under skin that was cold and clammy. His mother shifted haltingly to accommodate his head, and he wondered for a moment if this was the kind of pain she was in all the time, and how she could think of anything else if it was. Noah told her, "I love you," and he knew it was true, but all he really felt at that moment was, *This hurts, this hurts, this needs to stop hurting.*

"I love you too, my baby," Faye said, and Noah knew that it wasn't what she was thinking either, but he couldn't blame her. Her pain was his fault anyway; he understood.

8

WHEN RAY WAS TWELVE, TRACY had him on a strict reading schedule. A book
a week or two hundred pages (whichever came first) in four core subjects every
month: literature, history, science, and civics (or as it was put to Ray, current
events). Math concepts and piano lessons happened throughout the month,
but these reading projects took up most of his time. Literature he found the
least hateful, because at least sometimes the books had an interesting story,
and current events wasn't wholly bad—that was mostly news articles: war and
political scandals counted towards his page minimum. Science reading was the
worst. Sometimes Tracy would allow a series of documentaries in lieu of a book,
but very, very rarely.

Ray had to generate five pages of analysis a week based on his studies. It
was not really in addition to his regular homework, because almost any subject
coming from his teachers could be incorporated into Tracy's demands, but at a
certain point it became insulting to Ray. It wasn't as if he was some moron who
hated to read, so why did it have to be shoved so unpleasantly down his throat?

"Can't I pick a book I *want* to read?" Ray whined to her often, his body
going to noodles as he beseeched her from across the dining room table, where
after his first session he was made to sit always with his back to the window, so
there was no chance of his mind wandering to anything pleasant. "This isn't even
required for school or anything, it's just for, you know, my *enrichment*, right? So
why can't I pick sometimes?"

Tracy only took him seriously once, when she let him make up a list of
choices under each of her subjects for review. Every other time after that,
however, she threw her glasses down against that beaded chain and squeezed
the bridge of her nose, as if the question was so beyond stupid that it physically
pained her.

Ray had taken such care with that list too. He cleared a whole Saturday for
the preparation of it. Tommy was outside doing summersaults over a spitting
sprinkler, Allen and Eric were out at the movies probably with dates, his mother
was twittering away on the phone with her friends, planning some potluck

charity thing, and Ray was inside, like a *nerd*, compiling data.

His list was a research report in itself, as neat and thorough as one of Tracy's own syllabi. He left civics alone, since he didn't prefer a book on government powers or whatever to entreatingly short news articles from the paper. For science he picked a couple of popular books at the top of internet searches for space exploration, deep sea life forms, weapons manufacturing (*like guns, bombs,* he wrote, *related to world conflict, civics crossover?*), the lives of scientists like Einstein or astronauts, and maybe a book on code breaking and spying (although he knew this to be a long shot—spies were way too interesting to be educational).

History was an easier list. He liked World War II and apparently so did everybody else, because there was a glut of WWII books to be found, an embarrassment of countless riches. He listed books about the war, about the key players, about the true horror show: the secrets of the death camps. Being somewhat Jewish himself, he got a perverse shiver out of the subject, the same sort of feeling he got when looking at a swarm of insects, but amplified to human levels of revulsion. That was probably asking too much; real gore wasn't going to slip by Tracy.

Under literature Ray wrote up an extravagant Christmas list of titles. For detectives he just put down fictional names: Sherlock Holmes, Sam Spade, Peter Wimsey, whole series he could consume in no time. And cowboys, so many, and these could easily be history subject crossovers: Billy the Kid, Jesse James, Butch and Sundance, the O.K. Corral. Literature's a wide subject, right? It didn't just go Bible, Shakespeare, Dickens, Hawthorne, Melville, and then halt, right? He wrote down stuff that Tracy *must* embrace, like canonical, old stuff. An oldie but a goodie, that's how Ray thought of each topic he listed in the other third of his list: Edgar Allan Poe, Mark Twain, the Beat Generation, but even those mindful, conservative choices were shot down with the rest of them.

"Trash," Tracy said. "Violence and prurience, look that word up. These subjects were shallow entertainment in their own time, and they're the same today. It's not worth our time."

Ray crossed his arms and locked his lips between his teeth, holding in an outburst. *Our* time? Please. Tracy got paid for her time, and Ray's time was totally forfeit. His brothers were never drilled this hard, they were meatheads, morons, but Ray was cursed with *potential*. Potential he had to *fulfill*. So screw his time, his whole lifetime, apparently.

"Can I at least read this stuff in my *free* time?" he gritted at her.

Tracy smirked, and she spoke with relish when she said, "If you have enough free time for that sort of garbage, then I'm not doing my job."

Ray half-sneered back at her but stayed quiet. She baited him, she messed with him, she really did. Sometimes Ray could deal with it, like it was an inside joke between just the two of them, the smart ones. Not for his weight-lifting brothers, his function-flitting mother, or good old disappearing dad, just the people dialed in enough to get sarcasm, and back-handedness, and irony. But this casual send-off of Ray's wish list? Giving him just enough rope to hang himself, just for her own amusement? This wasn't about putting on a show for the family, this was private and this was personal.

This put him off Tracy for good.

9

WHEN NOAH WAS THIRTEEN HE became a man. His brothers bitched for weeks when they had to study for their bar mitzvahs, but Noah found the task of grasping a little Hebrew to be incredibly rudimentary. He was already perfectly fluent in English and German, and had even set himself a task as a child to learn the word for 'hello' in every single language. He had a knack for cataloguing and data organization that served him well in both his studies and his hobbies: languages, birds, coin collecting for a bit, and now geography (his aim at the moment was to memorize the capitals of every country).

The stuff at temple was no big deal, and Noah didn't have enough friends for a party, or enough optimism to try and have one anyway (somehow the kids at middle school found out he'd gone to a girl's school for a while, and that was it for friends until at least high school). The only real highlight of this occasion was the long-promised dinner with Dad. His brothers each got theirs: a whole meal, a real restaurant, one-on-one with Dad for the whole night. It would not be cancelled, it would not be rearranged, it would not be cut short. Noah had been left jealous twice as his father explained to them each time before: "This is important. This is the first time someone's expecting you to be a man, and with that expectation comes a certain level of respect." It was a dry pitch, but it was a big deal. Rumor from his brothers was that the occasion came with the option of trying some of Dad's wine, *and* he'd get to talk about himself the whole time without Dad's face freezing into that *I'm listening* manic, nodding grin.

Mom always assured Noah that Dad's incredibly fake listening face wasn't due to a lack of interest.

"He loves you kids, but he's just not a big fan of kids in general." Mom, accessible to talk to any time of the day or night, was letting Noah brush her hair the last time this talk occurred. "He's only anxious to find out who you're going to become." She smiled at him via her vanity mirror.

"Aren't I already who I'm going to be?"

"Well," she said, taking his hand and pressing her pale lips to the back of it, "I hope so."

Dinner with Dad was at the same restaurant in the city where he took major clients, the one where he treated Mom on special anniversaries, and of course the location of this father-son tradition.

Noah had heard about this place for most of his life. Aunt Clarice loved it for the famous people who could occasionally be spotted there, his father for the apparently world-class food, his mother for the ambiance of the room, the shimmer of it. She said it was like a carpeted ballroom in there, the perfect kind for someone who couldn't dance.

It was the light in the place that first impressed Noah when he walked in. There was a candle at every table, and low-hanging personal chandeliers above each one. The feel of the place was like being surrounded by a harmless fire, the lights orange and wavering, the floor a deep, plush ember.

A crisp maître d' lead them to their table. It was close enough to the front that Noah could hear a ringing phone sometimes, but it sounded mellow and unhurried. The menus were as fancy as diplomas. The food listed there was rich and exotic even to Noah, who grew up with very nice things. Eels and quail eggs and truffle shavings and caviar—food that used to be too good for him.

Noah ordered something French just for the joy it gave him to know how to pronounce it. As they waited, Noah Sr. gave his son the most genuine smile of his life.

"Thirteen," he said. "What do you think about starting high school next year?"

"Eh, it's only about a year of work, no big deal."

Noah Sr. laughed. "Still going to try to test out early, huh? I don't know why you're so eager to stop being a kid. Once you start being an adult you can never stop."

"Sounds good to me. I've been young my whole life, I'm sick of it," Noah said, mostly joking.

His father laughed again, almost a guffaw, as a woman brought their drinks and greeted Dad by name.

"Mr. Kaplan, a pleasure to see you again." She tucked the silver drinks tray under one arm and shifted her hips like a slide rule to stand and chat. "This is another junior Kaplan I assume?" she asked, nodding at Noah from the top of a long and powder-soft neck.

"You don't know how right you are, Sarah. This is Noah Jr., our youngest."

"I prefer Noah the Second," he told Sarah when she reached out to shake his hand. He had been waiting to say that for about four years. It made his father laugh all over again, but only made Sarah smile politely.

"Wonderful. Your entrees will be out shortly," she said, and left their table on slender heels that sank into the carpeting with every step.

"Mom would have thought it was funny," Noah murmured, eying his father's wine glass and still trying to decide if he wanted any. His brothers said it tasted like juice left out in the hottest sun for days, sour and acrid (though not in those words—those are words Noah found for himself after he smelled the top of an empty bottle after a party at home).

"Well, your mom's got a rare sense of humor, you can't expect everyone to understand you like she does." Dad picked up his wine glass and started to swirl it around . . . self-consciously? He was always careful when he talked to his children about their mother. "She used to crack herself up all the time when we first met, especially when nobody else got the joke. Her laughing made me laugh, and she says that's what made her like me so much at first, that I got her jokes."

"But you didn't."

"No, and I don't really get yours either, but you're both so funny when you try, you get that same cocky look on your face when you're about to deliver a punch line. You remind me of her the most." Noah nodded at his father; he already knew he was the most like Mom of anyone else in the family, even her sister. "Hey, it's time for your first real toast. Here, you take this," Noah Sr. said, sliding his wine glass discretely across the table and lifting a water glass for himself. "L'Chayim."

Noah took the wine glass, and felt that cocky look his father mentioned come across his face as he translated.

"To life."

10

When Ray was fourteen, he graduated from high school. He didn't turn a tassel over a mortarboard or walk through the ceremony, but he finished his classes, and got his diploma in the mail, and got accepted into college at the University of Chicago, so it was a done deal. He didn't really want to do it so early, and didn't really mean to, but every time Tracy saw an opportunity for Ray to test out of a class, she forced him to take it.

"If you pass this test, you only have to take one more required math class," she'd explain. Or she would say, "If you take this class at the school and take another just like it online, you could be done with your Social Studies credits in just one semester."

He knew he'd skipped his freshman year entirely, starting high school classes with the sophomores, and rising with them the next year as a junior, but he'd had no idea that Tracy was setting him up to graduate so quickly. One day over the winter break she came to him with both his parents in tow and laid out the whole plan:

"You'd have to really cram over this last semester, you'd be taking almost a double load of classes, but at the end you'd be *done*. And if you can manage it, your parents and I have agreed you should get a big reward."

Tracy turned to look at his parents, Mom and Dad standing stiffly side-by-side in a way that said clearly this wasn't their idea.

"A summer abroad," Dad said.

"Europe, somewhere nice," added Mom. "Please don't go picking anywhere war-torn."

"I'd get to pick?" Ray asked. Because every choice concerning him up until that moment had been inflicted upon him by everyone else.

"Yes," Tracy said, speaking up again as his parents returned to their own lives. "But you have to graduate first. It's incentive, you don't have anything yet."

So Ray buckled down. He practiced and re-practiced the SATs, he got all the signatures necessary for the special dispensation needed to graduate so unnecessarily early. He enrolled at the University of Chicago pending his successful graduation. He endured the loneliest semester of his life. He did most of his living in his head.

Picture yourself in Paris, he'd think before falling asleep. *Wine, art, architecture, cheese, poetry, can you see it? The joy of correcting everyone else's pronunciation of French words for the rest of forever?*

Picture yourself in Dublin, dude, he'd think the next night. *Rolling emerald hills, redheads, Guinness, literature . . . maybe you'd use lose your virginity to a girl with freckles on every inch of her skin?*

Picture yourself in London, picture yourself in Berlin, in Madrid, in Athens. Picture yourself gone from Chicago, somewhere in the sun.

He decided at long last on Italy, Venice or Rome or Naples, he didn't care. He'd pictured himself learning how to punt, or visiting the Coliseum, or walking hands-in-pockets through some piazza. He decided: *As long as I come home with an unstoppable tan, I'll have no regrets.* As long as he came home with stories of la dolce vita, la bella vita . . . the good life.

At last the calendar turned over to May. The paperwork was filed and his summer was wide open and free. He went to his mother with some prepared research: the best priced plane ticket for flying the nest at last, a few somewhat shabby but still safe hotels, pictures of all the places he would visit, information on how the tram lines operated, everything he could think of. All he needed to get the whole thing going was some money, one of the family's credit cards. He expected Mom to smile wistfully, touch his face, and hand it over.

"Oh, Ray," she said with a sigh as she ranged her eyes over all the print-outs on the same dining room table where Ray had sat studying for six solid years. "Look, you need to know, we never really thought you'd actually graduate so fast. You can be so lazy with your homework sometimes, Tracy said a goal might help motivate you, but really honey, you're only fourteen. Dad and I aren't going to let you go to another country, alone, for three whole months. Just because you managed to get through school so fast doesn't mean you're mature enough for that sort of freedom."

For a moment Ray didn't even process what she was saying. He was staring at his itinerary, and thinking, *Was I reading while she was talking and got the words mixed together?* But he replayed it in his head, and cocked his skull to see her looking down at the table sort of exasperated, wearing the same look she had when one of her jokes fell flat with her sons, like she thought they were old enough to get it by now, but boy was she ever wrong in expecting so much.

The burning feeling of being wronged erupted in his core and flooded through him, prickling the hair on top of his head and making his toes curl up in his shoes. It was the same intensity of every tantrum of his youth, but *goddammit* he wasn't a kid anymore! This really *wasn't* fair. He was promised something and the deal had just been reneged on. How long was it going to take to get some respect around here?

Ray felt his hands clench into fists, realized that he longed to bash his mother right in the face, and turned away before the urge overwhelmed him. He was heading fast for the front door to try and sprint the rage out of him before it became a destructive force; he would start breaking things soon, he could feel it, like a barometer plummeting before a violent storm.

"Can you please clear the table before you go off in a huff?" his mother called after him. "Other people live here and might like to use it, you know."

"Oh sure," Ray said through clenched teeth, returning quickly, feeling heady as his blood pressure dampened his hearing, making him both clear-headed and dizzy. "Let me get that."

He set his hand flat on the nearest page and swept as many as he could off the table and up towards his mother's irritated expression, then took off running away from her. He couldn't hit her, but she wasn't above slapping him.

"See?" she shouted after him. "This is exactly why you can't go! You're such a brat about everything."

Ray ran around the block a few times, no warming up and no stopping, and he let his muscles ignite as he fought the muggy spring air for enough oxygen to keep going as long as he was still angry.

He couldn't last it out. He went home angry, and woke up the next day angry, and stayed angry for weeks until he finally resigned himself to reality.

He adjusted his sights, set them on college, on spending the next year applying to ones out-of-state so he wouldn't be trapped in his parents' house any longer. The place felt like a prison to him.

But: *There are many confines, wards, and dungeons in the world,* he reminded himself, *and you're going to find a better one.*

FAST
FRIENDS

1

NOAH WAS QUICK TO LOSE friends and alienate others once he started attending college at the University of Chicago. He took the CTA to campus twice a week for classes, an eight-minute ride that he could have walked in about twenty minutes, but there were a million reasons not to do that: he'd show up sweaty, he'd ruin his nice shoes, he'd advertise that he lived at home with his parents, etc. He looked older than fourteen, but he'd always been small for his age, so it wasn't uncommon for people to figure out what it was that made him so odd. He was a kid to them, a child, a baby, and never mind that he set the grading curve for nearly every exam. No one talked to him for the first few weeks of classes, not until after the first test grades had been posted.

"Hey, why don't you join our study group, kid?" asked a tall black guy Noah later learned was named Omar. "You're always answering in class, you're smart. You hook us up, we'll hook you up, get you into parties, what do you say?" He was clearly speaking on behalf of his friends, a blond kid with a sharp nose and uneven eyes, and a carroty redheaded boy with burnt-looking freckles all over his face. Noah later discovered that these were Omar's roommates, Caleb and Ethan, but right away Noah could tell that Omar was the only one getting anyone into parties. Caleb had that drab, lopsided face and a pathetically old phone (so no looks and no money) and Ethan had the dumpling body of a young man that even wealth couldn't help, at least not in college. Omar had the unteachable ability to talk to anyone, including his dull roommates, and the classroom wunderkind.

Noah agreed to join their study group; he was so desperate to tell his mother that he was fitting in at college, literally any group would do. He didn't care if Omar was just bullshitting him, didn't care if he never saw the inside of a party, so long as they tolerated the title of Friends.

It was during their Legal Reasoning study sessions in the library that Noah first learned about Ray Klein.

"You know there's another really young guy who started this year too, do you know him?" Omar asked quietly during a snack machine break, six weeks into the semester. The softly crinkling wrappers made more noise than their conversation, but still they received glares from harried graduate students nearby.

"Oh, yeah," Noah said. "We're part of an invading horde, so we've obviously met at the tactical meetings."

The other guys laughed, but Omar only rolled his eyes and said, "Very funny."

"I think I spotted him earlier," Caleb said, stretching his neck to look around, bringing to Noah's mind the giraffe at the Lincoln Park Zoo.

"Look, there he is over there," Ethan said, pointing extravagantly enough to make this other boy look up from his study carrel and frown.

"I think he saw you," Omar said, knocking Ethan's arm out of the air with a light swat.

"I think you're right about that," Noah said. "Brilliant call."

Omar cocked his head to glare at Noah, which was the first moment Noah realized he was in the process of making an enemy. He admonished himself to lay off of Omar for the rest of the night, maybe even stop all casual conversation for that evening, and just stick to the homework.

"Ugh, he's a pretty boy," Caleb said, finally settling back into his box of a library chair and picking his pen back up. "You better hope he's got a shitty personality," he intimated to Noah. "'Cause, like, in the unlikely event that some girl can bring herself to molest one of you juveniles, it's going to be him and not you."

"Yeah, yeah," Ethan confirmed, coming back from rubbernecking. "He looks like a lady killer." And he did, even Noah could see that. He looked like he wore his clothes better than the mannequins that were first sewn into them.

"Yeah, like what's it called, like a chickenhawk or something," Omar said.

The group chuckle-mumbled over the word 'chickenhawk' for a few seconds, and Noah found himself faced with a profound dilemma: he'd just told himself not to antagonize Omar again that night, but he could never resist correcting people when they were wrong and he knew he was right. He'd even done it to his own dear mother on occasion; he couldn't not do it.

"He's not a chickenhawk, that's not what that word means," Noah released from his mouth.

"Fuck you," Omar said, "how would you know?"

"A chickenhawk is the one who preys on the young chickens, not the young one who gets preyed upon," Noah explained. "And it's mostly a gay term anyway: chickens are the young boys, and the hawks are the men." He came across the phrase while searching about hawks years ago, and the term stuck in his head.

"You're a mostly gay term," Ethan said, and quietly fist-bumped Caleb over grabbing that low-hanging fruit.

"But chickens would be women," Omar argued. "Otherwise why do we call them chicks? Chickens are women."

"They're really not," Noah said. "Look it up any time you like. Chicks are women, yeah, and hens are women, but chickens are boys, okay? And roosters, cocks, and chickenhawks? Those are all men. I know I'm right."

Omar's jaw clenched, and Noah realized that this was the end of the study group, though Caleb and Ethan did not. One of them started chanting *roosters, cocks, and chickenhawks,* and the other one joined in, and a library monitor came over and whispered that it was time for them to leave, that they were becoming disruptive.

Outside of the library—where the guys usually chatted for a bit, and frogged each other's arms, and waved goodbye to Noah, and promised to all meet again next week—this time Omar looked up chickenhawks on his phone, and in bitterness and defeat, he lit a cigarette too close to the doors.

He said to Noah, "You know too much about gay stuff."

And Caleb and Ethan winced to one another and looked at Noah like they were glad Omar said that to him and not them.

And Noah sighed deeply and said, "Well, good luck on the test, guys," before turning away.

All the way home he consoled himself with one thought: *You might have failed at making friends, but you're going to destroy them all on the test.* It went a long way in comforting him.

2

RAY MADE MORE FRIENDS AT THE University of Chicago, but he actually had it just as hard as Noah did at first, before he learned to read all the new patterns around him. He was also too young, younger than Noah even, *the* youngest student on campus. That title caused plenty of other students to feel either threatened by or dismissive of him. On top of that: he was too attractive, a problem Noah (with his bulging gaze and slumped shoulders and heavily connected brows) did not have. Ray had a naturally flattering part in his hair, distinct jaw and cheek bones, and an even, white smile. The other fellows especially seemed to think he should be smart *or* good-looking, but certainly not both. Whenever he answered honestly about how he'd come by college so early, he was met with an aura of disgust or offense, like it was morally suspicious to go through school that quickly.

So Ray stopped being honest again right away. It was foolish to have ever reverted to truth in the first place, but those early hectic days of class, the situation with his mother left unresolved and simmering so that his home life was uncomfortable too, and having to answer honestly on all his paperwork (just for simplicity's sake) . . . the old bad habit of truth-telling had come back to him. It was important to train it away once more. He struck gold in his second week as a university man when he heard himself say:

"How do you think I got to college so young? Obviously I slept my way to the top."

He used the line over and over, trying to escape the first pigeonhole everyone placed him in. Sometimes a guy would twist it into a gay joke, but Ray would only double down and pretend to flirt with the comedian if the guy was just being smart, or say, "It's okay to be jealous," if the comment had more self-defense about it. Sometimes a girl would frown about that being a sexist joke, and Ray would stop short, mimic her frown, and say, "Oh, yeah, I guess it is," and then keep his brow tense until she went away like her observation might be eating him alive with its implications.

Ray found he could diffuse or ignite any situation he was in. Secretly he was Prometheus, with the knowledge of fire, but to everyone else Ray made himself a perfect martyr to each arrow flung at him. Every joke at his expense he met with a face of ironic joy, every rebuke was taken in with as humble a stance as possible. Was he not here to laugh, was he not here to learn? And eventually everyone seemed to like him, or at least not particularly dislike him. Everybody, except for one.

Ray was aware of Noah before Noah was aware of him, several of his many new friends mentioned hearing about some young kid who was correcting professors and basically being a little smartass in some of the classes, and they would say, "At first I thought they were talking about you, but since when do you quote Nietzsche?" Ray did not, and no one had ever accused him of such a thing before. He made it his business to find out about this other genius kid. He wasn't worried about protecting his reputation so much as he was terribly curious. Could there really be another person even remotely comparable to himself? He didn't like to think so.

He had staked out Noah's study sessions for three weeks in a row before Noah finally noticed him; he wasn't in the library by accident. Ray did his studying at home when he did it at all, with Tracy still tutoring him, but at severely reduced hours, and getting more and more fed up with his laziness—she disapproved of his parents reneging on the promise of travel abroad (a trip that she would have accompanied him on, she wrongly assumed), but she was much more affronted by Ray's plummeting efforts to educate himself.

"I thought you had your own ambition, but I was wrong wasn't I?" she'd asked him a few weeks into the school year. Ray, who had been combing his hair with his fingernails in the reflection of his mother's china cabinet and thinking fondly of Narcissus, glanced sidewise at her and simply shrugged.

He kept a section of notebook about Noah, with everything he was able to discern from afar:

- doesn't really need those glasses, uses like prop
- does he ever wash his hair? looks so greasy
- lives off campus, still at home? then why so greasy?!
- I wouldn't roll my eyes if they were that big, only draws attention
- wears the same thing every day like a cartoon character
- books all labeled Kaplan, N.—school email search reveals: Noah F.
- Jewish—bar mitzvah announcement online—really didn't need that in common with him too
- studying law, definitely smarmy enough
- aha! he doesn't like me either—good

Ray was displeased when his cover was blown by Noah's table mates, but he had reached the limits of long distance observation anyway. The next step, if he chose to take it, would be investigation pertinent to possible contact.

Ray befriended Omar to find out what class he had with Noah, and from there Ray learned Noah's other classes because Noah stacked them all on the same two days a week, obviously to minimize his time spent on campus; he never came early, never lingered afterwards, and was never seen on the weekends. Not a coffee stop, not a snack at the vending machines, not even solo time in the library. He brought his own food, he reserved his books in advance for pick-up, he was the dullest person Ray had ever seen.

Ray would have had to stalk him to his bus stop to meet him 'naturally' or else literally run into him on 'accident,' and he hadn't seen anything interesting enough for that kind of effort, so he didn't expend it. His curiosity quenched (verdict: terminal nerd, not in the least like himself), he dropped Noah as a hobby and didn't think of him unless someone else mentioned him first, or gave another report of the kid's incredibly antisocial behavior.

Ray would say to them, "Oh, you've met my Mr. Hyde! I always seem to just miss him." The people would laugh, and Ray would forget Noah again. By winter break, Ray forgot the kid's real name, and no one else in his circle ever bothered to know it in the first place.

3

NOAH BELIEVED THAT HIS FIRST college party would also be his last. He knew what it would be without ever going: too loud, too juvenile even for him, probably cloyingly overcrowded, and he was right. A mulchy backyard, a lot of people not half as attractive as the college kids in movies, all burping and playing meaningless music, meaningless games . . . beer pong, truth or dare, courtship.

Noah found himself there because even his mother had started insisting he try some fun, saying, "You can't hate something you've never tried," same as she used to say to him about eating his vegetables. He wanted to trip her up, say something like, "What about anal sex? What about murder? Should I give those a shot too just to make sure I don't like them?" But he didn't smart back to his mother. First of all, she might smart right back at him ("How do you think your father and I met?"), and second of all she was right—it wasn't scientific of him to do no firsthand research before forming a theory.

So he went to a random backyard party in October, off-campus, thrown by a group of recent alums who couldn't let it go. He held a plastic cup but refused to drink from it. He rooted for his 'team' in the guys vs. girls beer pong battle but did not play. He kept checking his watch and wondering, *Is this long enough? Is this long enough?* He'd walked there and could leave for home at any moment, but he kept delaying. It wouldn't do to show up back home too early without enough details. He'd only be pressured to do it again if he didn't return with a full thesis on why parties just weren't for him.

The longer he stayed, the more he noticed a particular young man, the Chickenhawk as Noah had come to think of him, using the misnomer for convenience's sake, in spite of himself. No matter where Noah moved—painfully close to the speakers, or over by the coolers, or braving the inside for the kitchen covered with chip crumbs and mystery smears—this kid was in his periphery, a pale shirt of either white or blue, glowing faintly in the night like a preppy ghost.

In less than a year, Noah would look back at this moment and think of it fondly, fatefully, even though he remembers perfectly well how it began. He became frustrated at some point and spat at the Chickenhawk, "What!"

In lieu of introducing himself, Ray asked Noah, "Would you like to know why some people call you Mr. Hyde?" He held out a hand to shake. "I'm the reason."

Noah had shaken his hand without meaning to, and snatched it away when he realized they were touching.

"Yeah, well, you should hear what my friends call you."

Ray smiled. "I'm also the reason you're not going to be the youngest graduate of this place."

"You think so?" he asked.

"I'd certainly bet on it."

Noah said nothing to this, hoisted his cup up to block Ray's face and crossed his other arm over his body to prop up his elbow. He turned away thinking, *It has to be long enough now, I even talked to someone,* when Ray said, "Are you even drinking that? What is it?"

"No, I don't know, it was in a vat or something. Someone scooped it out and handed it to me. It's making my hand sticky."

Ray wafted a hand over Noah's cup, smelling the drink's bouquet. He wore a class ring that glowed under the low-hanging light strands strung up between tree branches.

"I believe the term is 'jungle juice.' Can I try some? I got here too late and they ran out."

"Take the whole thing, I haven't even touched it."

Ray accepted the cup, took one gulp and nearly gagged, then drank the rest with a few struggling chugs.

"Thanks, it was disgusting."

"Why did you drink it, then?"

"Because there are sober people in Africa."

"Sober people in Africa," Noah mumbled, nearly smiling. That's also something his mother used to say about vegetables, that people were starving in Africa or North Korea or the Middle East, and that it was wrong to turn up his nose at good food.

"You like that one? People usually like that one, it's a crowd pleaser."

"Are you trying to be a comedian?" Noah asked, realizing that he was having a whole conversation and looking forward to the end of it, so he could go home and tell the family.

"I'm trying to make friends, and all the world loves a clown."

"Okay."

There was a lull. Noah looked his partner in interaction up and down so he could give his mother the details: the boy was another prodigy, dressed well and probably from a good family, very easy-going and friendly, handsome (his mother would know what he meant; open-faced, athletic). She'd want to know his actual name.

"So what's your name?" Noah asked, just as he was being asked, "So why are you in college so young?"

"Raymond Klein."

"Because I'm really smart."

"How smart? Were you tested? I have a genius IQ."

"Immeasurably smart. I'm literally off the chart."

"And humble too!"

Noah opened his mouth to say that being humble is for the inferior when someone in a circle of pot-smokers vomited over the back of her plastic lawn chair, dangerously near Noah's feet. The more gallant of the smokers got up to help her. Noah turned to leave.

"I'm done here, I never meant to stay long enough for puking."

"I live nearby, want to go back to mine?" Ray asked, accompanying him through two backyards and out to the sidewalk. "I know where my brother keeps a stash of booze."

"I live near here too, and I don't really want to drink after that display."

"Walk you home then?"

"Yeah, fine."

They walked in silence for three blocks, Noah trying to think of something polite to say that was in no way an invitation. He'd reached his limit for the night of social stimulation.

"This is me," Noah said as they approached his mailbox, which displayed 4754 S. Greenwood Ave. in little hanging signs.

"We're neighbors," Ray said. "I'm just over on Ellis."

"Then I'm sure we'll meet again." Noah stopped and held out his hand again. "By the way, I'm—"

"Kaplan, Noah F., I just remembered." Ray shook his hand with gusto.

"That's weird that you know my name."

"And you're address too, now. See you around."

With that Ray saluted Noah, and walked on.

4

Ray lobbied for Tracy to be fired just days after he formally made Noah Kaplan's acquaintance. It used to be that Ray was accountable to her only, and whatever infractions he committed were dealt with in-house, but college changed all that. She had no real control over him anymore—he knew it and she knew it, and he started disobeying her in overt ways, not doing her extra assignments, and not meeting her standards for his homework. His grades slipped a bit, yes, but for such a young man in his first year of college, no one batted an eye at Bs and Cs. In fact, everyone but Tracy praised him for holding his head up so well when he was so far out of his depth. She knew he could do better, and so did he, but why should he waste the effort? It all came out in the wash anyway. If he got Cs all through college, he still got the same degree as everyone else, and had enough time for some fun while he was at it.

"You really need to show me you can refocus," she said as she packed up her ridiculous backpack covered in zippers, as if she might be headed out hiking at any moment. "I realize you're more independent these days, a big man on campus, but now is the worst time to start slacking off. What you do in your first year will set the tone for the rest of your college career, and you don't want to look back and know that just a little effort now would have saved you a whole lot of struggle in the long run."

He was barely listening to her. He knew about this party, the announcement was sent to the whole student body—not an official school function, but some people who had kept their house off-campus sent it out, especially to new freshmen, to welcome them. Most of the people Ray knew weren't going to be there; they were forming their own groups and didn't want to know a bunch of graduated adults, but Ray prided himself on being comfortable in any group of people. After all his time alone, studying under Tracy's thumb, he couldn't get enough friends, or enough parties.

"I want you to study this weekend. I want you to have this work done by our Monday session. It's important."

But Ray knew that wasn't true, and so he made a list of what he actually had to do to avoid failing, and tossed all of Tracy's extras in the foot well under his desk, to rest his feet on.

He went to the party (scraggly, sparse, sad, barely better than studying), and managed to spot Mr. Hyde aka Noah Kaplan, and at long last there was no one better to talk to, so Ray watched him, and provoked an exchange, and became intrigued.

This kid was no liar; he didn't have the finesse for it . . . but an off the charts IQ? If he was so smart, why couldn't he fit in? Why come out if he wasn't going to try? Why take a cup and not drink from it? Fascinating.

Ray ended up home early that Saturday night, but let the party punch put him to bed. He didn't do anything but his actual homework on Sunday night. Monday evening came around and he had nothing more than a few pages to show Tracy for his English class. She got so pissed she threatened to go to his mother. Ray called her bluff.

"Let's go," he said, "let's find my mother right now." He got up from the dining room table, and she followed, as dogged a poker player as himself.

Anna wasn't in the kitchen (no surprise there), nor in the rest of the downstairs rooms. Ray bounded up the steps, Tracy following with a sigh and a crackle of knees. They found Anna in Dad's office twittering away on the phone about gossip (not business), legs up in his overlarge burgundy leather chair, bare feet at the end of her slacks tucked underneath her.

She held up a finger to keep them both silent until she could extricate herself from the call. After hanging up, she tied her hair back before turning to them and raising an open hand.

"Tracy's extra work is actually distracting me from my studies," Ray said first. "She's not helping me anymore."

"I know he has a lot more work now that he's in college, but it's no more than he's used to. It is harder material, much harder, and his grades have slipped because of it. In my opinion he does still need a tutor, now more than ever to keep him on task."

"So I can go to college, but I still need a nanny? I can go to my classes and sit for exams and attend parties"—at this Tracy sighed—"but I can't go to Europe," Ray said looking sidelong at his tutor, "and everyone still knows better than me what I need?"

Anna pressed her eyes briefly and told her son, "Don't work yourself into a rant, Raymond. Tracy is on a yearly contract, we can't just fire her, which is obviously what you want. But you've got a point, it's probably time to let you sink or swim, so Tracy . . . I think we won't be able to renew your contract after this year."

Tracy nodded her understanding. Ray smirked and said, "Finally."

"You still have to listen to her for the rest of the year, I'm serious. Nothing has changed yet. And Tracy, if you want I can ask around for anyone who might need a tutor of your caliber. Of course you'll get excellent recommendations from us."

"Right; I would appreciate any referrals."

Anna nodded perfunctorily and Ray and Tracy turned to leave. Outside the door of the office, Tracy drawing it shut behind them, they looked at each other.

"Your English paper needs work," she told him, and moved past him to lead the way downstairs. Ray set his hands on the banister and watched her go, feeling victorious, but not feeling the need to gloat about it. He had won, and Tracy acknowledged it, and satisfaction fell over him with a languid warmth. It rolled down his body like an unfurling cape.

5

FOR HALLOWEEN THAT YEAR, NOAH stayed at home to hand out candy with his mother. He had stayed at home the year before, and the year before that. A few times as a kid she walked him around the block to collect candy for himself, but she could barely manage those short excursions, and soon Noah didn't see the point of it. He could dress up at home, there was candy at home, why not just stay at home?

They set a couple of the iron chairs that usually sit on the back patio out on the sidewalk in front of their gate. Faye held (and grazed from) a bowl of candies with chocolate, Noah held a bowl of candies without. They kept a line of color commentary going on which costumes were best, and bestowed their favors accordingly. Noah wore plastic vampire fangs, a bloody bit of drool drawn by lipstick, and had blacked a widow's peak onto his forehead with some eyeliner. Faye wore a white-striped fright wig and a lipstick bite wound on her neck. Noah was up and down, back and forth all evening—for candy refills, coffee, jackets—keeping his mother comfortable as the sun went down.

Just when it was turning full dark, Ray showed up.

"Good evening beautiful madam, young sir," he said, walking with a guiding hand on the head of a little boy, no bigger than kindergarten.

"What do we have here?" Faye asked the child, who was dressed as a pirate. He had a plastic cutlass tucked in his belt, a lunch box shaped like a treasure chest into which he collected his edible loot, and a small tricorn hat with a Jolly Roger insignia patch sewn on one side, and a small stuffed parrot tucked into the corner of the other.

"I'm Jack Sparrow!" he announced.

"And you two are . . . Bela Lugosi and Morticia?"

"Lily Munster, notice the skunk stripes," Faye corrected him, as Noah handed the pirate boy a few candies off the top, watching this interaction carefully. He had still not decided that Ray was worthy, and he was very protective of his mother.

"Ah, very pleased to meet you, then," he said taking and lifting her hand towards him, though not being presumptuous enough to kiss it.

"And who are you supposed to be?" she asked Ray.

"Hmm, must be . . . Eddie Haskell!"

Faye laughed hard enough to surprise herself, wincing at the end of the yelp because she hadn't braced her midsection, hadn't been ready for it.

"If you don't know Lily Munster, you're way too young to know who Eddie Haskell is."

"I'm too young for a lot of the things I know, isn't that right, Noah?"

"Oh, yes." Noah wakes out of the trance he had been in watching Ray charm his mother. "Mom, this is Ray Klein, the one I told you about who's at school with me. My age, lives nearby?"

"And this is Tommy," Ray said, gesturing towards his brother, who gazed longingly at the kid-swarmed street.

"Here, have an extra treat for being so patient, Tommy," Faye said, handing over more candy. "You'll have to come by sometime soon," she told Ray, "when you can stay and chat a while."

"Sure thing. I'm sure Noah will invite me any day now."

"Huh? Yeah," Noah said, as Tommy finally became fed up with niceties, took his brother by the finger, and dragged him away.

"Goodnight," Ray called as he left.

"Goodnight," chorused Noah and Faye.

Faye sighed extravagantly, more energized than she'd been all night, her posture straighter and her eyes more open.

"He's a whirlwind, isn't he? Do you know him well?" she asked her son.

"We met at that party," Noah told her. "You know . . ."

Faye nodded as they say together, "The one." The only one.

Noah put his fingers, gone cold from holding the metal armrest of his chair, on the back of his neck, which was now feeling very hot.

"That might be nice, having someone your own age at school. Looks like he could bring you out of that shell of yours." She reached to pinch the air in front of his cheek, a gesture of a gesture.

"What if I'm a turtle? My shell is my skeleton; I'll die if I leave it."

"Your shell is an egg, okay? Emerge already."

"You just think my friend is cute. Please don't be that mom."

Faye hiccupped another laugh, not as vigorous as the one Ray coaxed out of her, but enough to assure Noah that his place was not about to be usurped.

They spent another hour and a half outside, Noah going in once to make them hot cocoa, since winter was coming on strong that year, with snow slated to arrive in early November. He and his mother both disliked winter especially. Some people in Chicago enjoyed the snow for at least the first few weeks, but Noah and Faye did not.

With full darkness finally fallen, a much colder breeze swept up the street, making Faye shiver. Noah stacked the candy bowls together, light enough for his mother to carry in, and he dragged the patio chairs to the backyard, thinking bitterly of the coming winter, until his thoughts turned to Ray.

He bore a striking resemblance to the best friend Noah imagined he'd have by this age. Someone strong, commanding, golden, who appreciated the best in Noah, and *wanted* him around. He'd passed close to that kind before—he thought Omar was a possibility for a bit, and there was another boy in middle school who'd showed Noah how to find porn on the internet, that kid seemed pretty worldly at the time—but those friendships hadn't been anywhere near as enduring as he'd hoped they would be. His friends were never as vibrant as they seemed on first interaction.

He decided to keep an open mind though, when he went in for the night and saw his mother still cheerful, humming "This Is Halloween" softly as she made her evening tea (for swallowing down her evening meds). If Ray Klein could make her smile while doing that, he must be something special.

6

Two weeks into November, Ray and Tracy had another nasty spat, an occurrence more and more frequent as her tenure in the household slowly expired. Ray stormed out halfway through the session, tired of being picked at just because Tracy was pissed off. He snatched his jacket on his way outside, but was too incensed to remember his phone, his keys. He found himself stranded in his front yard, too prideful to go back inside, and he started walking, assuming rightly, that he would figure something out by the time he made it around the block.

He knew he would try Noah's house after he turned his first corner, taking in huge brisk lungfuls of fall air, whistling a bit at the promise of something new to do. He felt sure that Noah would be home, remembering the kid's pathetic schedule, and he was right about that, too.

"Oh, yes, Noah's home. You're the boy from Halloween, right?"

Mrs. Kaplan, "Faye, I insist," invited him in with what at first looked like a hint of a bow, but as she continued to move, Ray noticed that her stoop stayed with her. Out from under the fright wig, her dim brown hair was tucked away into a squashed bun, and her cheeks, though strikingly prominent, were wan.

"I'd yell for Noah, but I might pass out," she told Ray, walking directly back to a little nest on the living room couch—blankets and food detritus and a trashy book. "Just go on upstairs, he's in his room, you'll find it."

This liberty was agreeable to Ray. He lingered over the family photos that hung along the stairs, trying to pick out every appearance of his new friend. He noted the interior design differences; someone in this house clearly didn't find walls of dark cherry wood oppressive. Ray's house was mostly pale marbles and cool blues, more reminiscent of a bathhouse. There were two closed doors, a bathroom, and a hallway on the second floor. The hallway appeared to lead to a more master area of the plane, if not a bedroom than an office. Ray decided to knock on both closed doors at once, hoping that Noah would emerge from one.

"How are you here?" was the first thing Noah said.

"Your mom told me to just come up and find you," Ray said, stepping into the room even though Noah had made no movement to invite him in. He wanted to see Noah's room in its untouched, unconscious state.

The books on the hutch above Noah's desk, and the ones lining his dresser, and the ones stacked up underneath his imposing four-poster bed, all looked boring as shit, and Ray communicated this.

"These books look boring as shit. Don't you read anything fun?"

"No," Noah said, accommodating Ray's invasion by moving into the room with him. Ray bounced down on the bed, while Noah rotated his desk chair and sat down somberly, like a doctor with an exuberant patient who doesn't yet know there's bad news. Noah wore the same buttoned-up outfit he wore on school days, even though Ray knew that it was not one of his school days.

"Do you ever *do* anything fun?"

"Not really. Most things considered fun are frivolous. I don't enjoy the feeling of accomplishing nothing."

Ray smiled. Noah told the truth as naturally and unabashedly as Ray told lies. He'd make a terrible alibi.

"Did you have a tutor growing up, is that why you're in college already?"

"I had a nanny who started me in school early, and then I skipped a few grades on my own."

"Why?"

"Why not? The material was easy, and the experience of being in lower education was not one I wanted to savor."

Ray paused to underline a few things he knew about Noah, really underline, and highlight: unpopular, but not insecure about it; mouth like a dictionary.

"I have a tutor. She gets fired at the end of this year, but right now she's still here, busting my balls."

"My nanny was a very large, strict German woman, I'm not sure I have sympathy for you."

"Just before I came over here," Ray said, sitting up straight to take on the challenge of gaining this boy's sympathy, "she told me, she said, 'It's mind-numbing trying to punch up your sub-par homework from C minus to B, it's work a TA would be too good to do.' And she always holds her hand up just like she's got an invisible wine glass,"—Ray demonstrated this—"pontificating."

"You get C minuses?"

"My grades are fine, she exaggerates. You're just lucky you don't have someone breathing down your neck anymore."

"I breathe down my own neck. I want to be Harvard Law by the time I'm twenty."

"For Christ's sake, why?" Ray put his hands behind his head and leaned back against the nearest bedpost. "What's your hurry?"

"You've met my mother. She's sick, she's been sick since I was born. I want her to see me accomplish something. I can have fun later, if I so desire."

"You won't be young later."

"I don't feel young now. I'm an old soul, I've been told."

"Hmm." Ray pursed his lips, even started to fidget, as he waited to begin his next conversational gambit. Noah only sat across from him, stoic as a beetle. "What are your plans for Thanksgiving? Because we have a great house we go to every year, in Charlevoix. That's in Michigan."

"I know that. We go to my grandmother's every year."

"Hmm."

In the following silence, Ray stroked a toy hawk mounted to the nearest bedpost, like a scarecrow feature, a hell of a thing to want watching over you as you try to fall asleep.

"Next week though, it's my birthday," Noah volunteered. "And I always get my favorite food for dinner, and presents, and I'm allowed to invite a friend. Are you free on the nineteenth?"

"You don't already have a friend lined up?" Ray teased, jovial because at last he seemed to have cracked this nut.

Noah tilted a skeptical look at him, but smiled as he turned back to his desk. "Dinner is at six. It won't be kosher, and if you're allergic to peanuts, you can't have dessert."

"There are no restrictions on me," Ray said, standing and stepping to the door. "Keep your evening free after dinner, I have an idea for a present."

"Wait, what kind of idea?" Noah asked, twisting around in his chair. "Because I have class the next day."

"No, you don't, you're going to be sick that day," Ray said. He knocked on Noah's doorframe twice as he was leaving, and called back, "Trust me."

7

NOAH EXPECTED TURNING FIFTEEN TO feel utterly meaningless, and to pass without any big to-do. He couldn't drive yet, he wasn't young enough to get excited over cake or presents (he did get a nice leather notebook for his collection of bird sightings, and a not-a-phone, not-a-computer thing for class). Birthday dinners usually meant the same three things: the main dish would involve steak, the vegetable would not be carrots, and afterwards there'd be a cake. Hooray.

Ray showed up right on time looking nice, his hair combed down with something slick, a present tucked under his left arm allowing him to shake hands with his right, first with Noah (which Noah found awkward), and then with Noah's father (which went a lot smoother). There were four places set at the table.

"Don't you have brothers?" Ray asked as he sat down.

"They're older," Noah said.

"Sam is at college, up at Northwestern, and Mike just got a job downtown, entry level, but he's on his way," Noah Sr. said.

"Not like this one, right?" Ray said, seating himself in one sliding movement, as Noah struggled to inch his chair over the carpet. "Fifteen years old and not even president yet, the bum."

Faye and Senior laughed, and looked fondly at Noah. So accomplished, and now a funny friend! A friend who dominated dinner with stories of his brothers, acting out pranks so theatrically that he almost fell out of his chair once, but it was charming of him, to be so enthusiastic. He was acting his age, something Noah had long ago ceased to do.

As dessert wrapped up, Ray slid his gift over the table cloth as Faye said, "Oh, how sweet."

Noah knew he was holding books right away (all his aunts give him books, but never with any thought to what *kind* of books Noah actually reads). Ray revealed a bit more creativity with his choices.

To Kill A Mockingbird, *The Maltese Falcon*, and *Harry Potter and the Order of the Phoenix*. The first two were slim paperbacks, the third, a behemoth. What the French call 'un pavé,' a paving stone, and what Americans might call a roach killer.

"It's because I know you like birds, get it?"

Noah nodded and said thanks and set the books aside. He wouldn't get it until later that night, after he and Ray were left alone, and Ray said, "Let's go for a walk. Bring Harry Potter."

"Here, look," Ray said, taking the book from Noah's arms as soon as they passed under the first street lamp on the chilly autumn street. "Here's your real present."

Ray opened the book like a waiter uncovering a plate, flipping the front cover and about half an inch of glued together pages with one light flick, and presenting the heavier half with a flourish. The book had been hollowed out, a rectangle excised from the center of the pages, holding a big shiny flask.

"What's in it?"

Ray dug it out. "Gin, I think you can handle it."

Ray was right. It made Noah feel like he was drinking mouthwash, but he could still drink it, and soon enough he began to like it. He felt deft yet clumsy at the same time. Ray began to giggle.

"Oh, look," Ray said as they passed a house with bricks lining their flower beds. He bent dramatically to pick one up and pulled Noah quickly away from the scene of the theft. They rounded a corner and Ray started examining cars, choosing. "This is something I've been meaning to try."

"Un pavé," Noah told him, making a reference to his earlier thought, not fully aware that Ray would not and could not get it.

"You're drunk," he told Noah. "That's so cute, you've barely had any." He took another swig of the flask, handed it to Noah, took a pitching stance, and threw the brick at a car window. The brick bounced off, leaving a small scratch. Ray picked it up and urged Noah to 'cheese it,' laughing so hard he could barely get the words out.

"Did you just say 'cheese it'? *You're* drunk, who says that?"

"I picked it up from a book somewhere. Here, you try."

"Why are we doing this?" Noah asked, taking the brick unthinkingly as Ray traded him for the Harry Potter book.

"It's an experiment. I've looked up how to break side windows on cars, sometimes people have to, to save a dog or a baby or their keys or whatever, but it's hard, all the windows are crash rated now, it takes a really specific angle and amount of force, and I've tried a few times, but I can't ever break one."

"What's the point of this experiment? You know the windows can break, and that one eventually will. This experiment would not get funded."

Ray bent double laughing at Noah's logic, dislodging a lock of his hair, which hung dashingly over his forehead for the rest of the evening.

"The point is the experience, okay? I want to see if I can do it myself."

"Well, then, here." Noah set the brick on the book held securely in the crook of Ray's arm. "If that's the point, then I can't do it for you." He didn't want to smash anyone's window. He didn't care particularly about his neighbors' property, but there was still no point in it for him.

Ray scoffed, but was still smiling when he said, "Chicken."

"Name-call all you want; your reasoning is flawed."

"Nerd," Ray said to him, laughing again.

Ray threw the brick at a few more car windows as they circled back towards their houses, Noah getting more and more paranoid about being seen and getting caught each time. Ray never managed to break one, and eventually chucked the brick into someone's hedge, giving up for the evening.

"You still going to class tomorrow?" Ray said at the corner where they would part for the night.

Noah looked at his watch, couldn't see it worth a damn in the dark, and answered, "I'm going to try."

"Drink water before you go to sleep, then." Ray held out his hand for a goodbye shake. "Happy birthday."

"Thanks," Noah took the hand, and was thrilled when Ray pulled him closer for a very dudely one-pat, no-real-body-contact hug. In fact, that semi-hug was the best gift he'd gotten all night.

8

AT THE END OF RAY'S first semester, he received some good news he'd forgotten to wait for. Ray applied to transfer to one school in each state bordering Illinois, including Michigan across the lake. He figured a neighboring state was just far enough away for freedom, but still close enough that his mother might actually let him go. He didn't really like the schools in Iowa, Kentucky, or Missouri (they were not at all on par with the prestige of the University of Chicago), so he ignored their acceptances in favor of sticking it out in Chicago, with his new friend who helped make home less of a stifling bore. The schools in Milwaukee and Indianapolis refused him, but at last the letter from Michigan arrived just before Christmas, an early gift: assuming Ray kept his grades at a B average or higher for the Spring semester, he was welcome. He could be a wolverine, the letter said; a phoenix no more.

Last day of term: the yards were snowy but the sidewalks salted and clear for walking, and he found his acceptance in the mail box when he checked it on arriving home. The snow stacked on top of their mailbox was thick, tall, sculpted, like shampooed hair. It slid off with an audible plop when Ray slammed the little hinged door shut with satisfaction. He loved seeing that word at the top of a letter, *Congratulations*.

Two nights later: Ray finally put a brick through someone's car window and left it lying in glittered glass on their back seat. His success so startled him that he ran, scurrying and tripping, a full two blocks away. He cooled himself and circled back, and passed close enough to see a man in a bathrobe looking at the window with his hands on his hips. Ray didn't approach him, but imagined what he'd say if he did ("Oh shit, is that your car, what happened?"), and he reviewed what flick of the wrist/angle of the brick finally brought him such success, and he decided that the next time it happened, he would keep his head, and at least rob the glove box.

Christmas Eve: Eric was home after a ski trip with his college friends, bonding with Dad about the experience because they were the only two family members who had been on the slopes. Allen would arrive the next day in time for Christmas dinner, having spent Christmas Eve with his girlfriend's family in Skokie. The girlfriend would be coming too. Ray's mother was on the computer half the time looking at pictures of the girl, and at the coffee table half the time with baby albums, looking at Allen. She couldn't seem to decide if she was happy or sad that her first born was in a serious relationship. She was so distracted that Ray was able to dip into the adult eggnog without her noticing.

Christmas Day: it was seeing how Allen and Eric were treated that finally decided Ray on his acceptance to U of M. Once their sons went away and came back, Ray's parents treated them with such friendliness. No more trying to mold them, no more criticism, because too much nitpicking might drive their young men away forever. "As long as you're happy, we're happy," they said. "Let us know if you need any help." It needed to be done, getting out of the house. There was no reason to delay.

New Year's Eve: Noah's household didn't do anything for New Year's Eve but watch the ball drop, and at Ray's there was always a party. Ray invited Noah, said he'd come by and loiter at the Kaplan house while his mother was setting up (according to Anna, Ray still had the capability to be underfoot while she worked), and it was then that he told Noah about his choice first, before anybody else.

"Hey, so, I'm not going to be here next year," he told Noah as he sorted through the kid's closet for what should be worn to the party. Noah had a pitiful variety, probably because his mom was too unwell to shop for him. "I'm transferring to the University of Michigan."

Noah's heavy brows lowered, and gathered into a frown. He was sitting on the edge of his bed, clinging to his scarecrow freaky hawk post. "What for?"

"I applied before I met you, because my parents wouldn't let me go to Europe last summer. I had to get out of that house and away from them. I still have to do that."

"Hmm." Noah stayed very stiff as Ray held up two incredibly similar shirts in front of him. "U of M has a good law program."

"Ugh, I'd sooner go into medicine than law, and blood makes me puke."

Noah's frown deepened. "Neither of those fit me."

"Wait, you mean you! You study law." Ray tossed the shirts on the floor and squatted down over them to be on Noah's level. "You're thinking you'll come with me, you totally should! We could be roommates. It would be awesome!

"Maybe."

"Oh my God, you can at least apply, right? Think about it for a while, but apply right now. Today! Let's do it now."

Ray nudged Noah's computer awake, put down all his open spreadsheets and study notes and shit that he shouldn't have open over winter break anyway, and brought up the transfer application page for U of M.

"Fine," Noah said, pulling himself up and sitting down at the desk.

"You won't regret it," he said, patting Noah's sloped shoulders, and smiling, sure about his decision.

At midnight: Ray was looking forward to the brand new year, and bold on some more champagne than anyone intended to give him, he kissed Noah on the cheek and brought a mottled blush to his pallid face.

On New Year's Day: Ray broke the news to the family, and greeted the new year with a shining optimism. His life was about to begin.

9

NOAH COMPLETED THE TRANSFER APPLICATION to Michigan. It was all Ray could talk about once he got in, and Noah wanted to join in his sunny speculation as their spring term started in the middle of a long, dark, sturdy Chicago winter.

Noah did a little idle studying of maps and pictures of the Michigan campus on his own some nights, did the work of imagining a parallel version of himself, and seeing that Noah in the dorms with Ray, really leaving home, really doing it. That Noah had his feet up on some dirty laundry, was learning how to smoke all kinds of things, had started listening to music in earnest, like it mattered. That Noah was carefree, cool, truly young.

"Have you heard yet?" Ray asked every time they met after the deadline for Fall term transfers passed, after February 1st. And when Noah said no, Ray would inform him of another aspect of his plan:

Swinging into an empty seat on the bus he would say, "If we go together, we can room together, if not I'm going out for a fraternity, I think. My father was in some stuffy house when he was in college, I'll have to look around and pick one I can stand. I'm just too charming to keep to myself."

Meeting in the student lounge after their Tuesday classes with cups of hot coffee around which Noah warmed his freezing-red fingers, Ray would tell him, "Once you've found out you're in, don't worry, I've already thought about everything we need to pack. My brothers left a bunch of stuff behind after they graduated—mini fridge, microwave, extra-long single bed sheets, we'll have everything, and we're close enough to come home if we have to, but . . ." He'd lean close to Noah and touch his shoulder and look him straight in the eyes, and say, "Let's not have to."

Yanking on Noah's canary scarf whenever he spotted him trudging through snow on his own, Ray would say, "It snows like this in Michigan, but it doesn't feel as cold, no lake effect." And when Noah would frown at him, thinking, *Cold is cold, could a few miles really matter that much?* Ray would nod at him and smile and say, "Trust me, you can really tell the difference."

But most of Noah's speculation concerning Michigan revolved around what he would tell his mother if he got in. He couldn't tell her the real reason, that the thought of staying at home in Chicago without the first real friend he'd had in years was nearly unbearable. He and Ray had started riding to school together after New Year's—driving if the weather was particularly unpleasant, taking the bus the rest of the time. The sight of someone waiting for him on the corner, flicking a cigarette into the street so it wouldn't be in the way of all he wanted to say . . . Noah couldn't let that get away from him. Not getting into U of M, that was one thing, that was just life as Noah had become accustomed to it, that was out of his control. But if he did get in—and his grades were *way* better than Ray's, he knew—then Noah would be the one to say yes or no. Choosing to wake up in Chicago every day and walk out to meet nothing and no one . . . he'd hate himself forever. Having Ray around was like having an old constant ache suddenly removed. Noah hadn't realized how much pain he'd been in until it was gone, and he couldn't let himself get used to it again.

He'd tell her it started as a lark, then he'd explain the etymological origins of the term lark, from skylark, and how it most likely entered the lexicon as a term for playing about because of sailors who saw the birds darting about in their ships' rigging. Then he'd tell her: home was wonderful, but the college experience was important. Chicago was wonderful, but Michigan had a great placement rate for graduate school. She was wonderful, but Ray was too, and she was a sure thing, but Ray was now or never. She'd have to understand.

So in March the snow started to patch away and disappear. In March his mother began speculating about when the tulips would emerge. In March the letter came letting Noah in on his acceptance to the school in Michigan, and so in March, Noah told his mother that he'd be leaving in September.

Faye was propped up in her bed playing on an abandoned video game console of Sam's, focused on some game that looked like an Impressionist painting, and revolved around the premise of getting keys into locks, bricks into blocks; a game sold as a puzzle that could keep its players sharp. Noah brushed the bottoms of his feet off on his pant legs before he crawled in with her, settling onto newly laundered white bedding, stiff like thoroughly whipped heavy cream, and just starting to smell like her.

"You know Ray's transferring schools," he began. She did of course, because Ray had told her about it at least five times already. "Well, he got me to apply with him, and of course I got in, and I was thinking I might go."

Faye's player on the screen started long-jumping for no reason, arcing slowly, artfully, uselessly as it ran along. She was definitely listening.

"They have a great placement rate for law school, and it's only four hours away by car. I'll take the bus if Dad can't drive me there for orientation, obviously. Ray drives around on his permit, but you know I don't, but I'll have my license by Thanksgiving, and for Christmas, you know, so I can drive us home for all of that. I think it would be an adventure," he concluded. That was how Ray always billed it: an adventure, the first of many.

Faye smiled in the watery glow of the TV, paused her game, and shifted her shoulders towards Noah so that only half of her face was lit by the blue-green glow.

"I want you to be happy, and I want you to go for what makes you happy. Don't worry about me," she assured him. "I'm not going anywhere."

10

THE END OF THE SCHOOL year for Ray brought the end of the reign of Tracy. On her last day Mother handed Tracy an envelope with a cash bonus and a gift card someone else had given Mr. and Mrs. Klein at a fundraiser, and Ray shook her hand over-firmly, and she hefted her backpack out their door for the very last time.

"Your grades haven't been what we've come to expect anyway," Mother said as the door clicked closed. "She hardly deserved the amount we gave her, but I guess I could think of this last year as a form of charity. She was *clearly* out of her depth once you got into college work. She went to some rural school; I should have expected it."

"You should have listened to me, I told you," Ray said rotely as he went upstairs to gather his keys, wallet, and phone.

"You don't have to keep harping on it now, she's gone," Mother replied with the same tired familiarity. With Ray's departure to Michigan a sure thing, the fight had gone right out of their rivalry.

Ray went straight to Noah's house with a cheap bottle of wine he picked because the name Smoking Loon made him snort. He smuggled it in his now unused backpack out of the corner-cabinet vintages his parents kept for unimportant guests. He presented it to Noah upon entry to his room.

"It's not even one in the afternoon," Noah said.

"I'm finally without supervision, I can't help myself. Let's go drink this in the park like bums."

"We can't drink it out of that, unless we want to get arrested like bums too."

In the kitchen pouring wine into a large plastic squeezy bottle is where Faye found them. Ray saw her first, felt a presence come to stand just outside the doorway, and when he turned to look, she was smiling tolerantly at them.

Ray did an exaggerated slide to put his body between Faye and her view of the wine bottle. "We aren't drinking underage! I mean, uh, hello Mrs. Noah's Mom."

"I should stop you, but it's just so nice seeing you have fun," she said, speaking to them both, but looking only at her son.

"It won't all fit," Noah told her, stopping his pouring and capping the squeeze bottle.

"Want a hit off this?" Ray asked, taking the excess to Faye. She upended the bottle and finished it in three gulps.

"I'll hide this from your father," she said to Noah as he zipped their portion into Ray's backpack and handed it over. Ray slung it on and started moving towards the back door. Noah came with him taking a set of keys from a set of hooks shaped like keys (in case you got confused about what should go there). "Stay out of trouble, you two."

"I will," Noah promised her, backtracking to give his mother a kiss on the cheek.

"No promises," Ray told her as he held the door for her son and then closed it behind them.

Noah took in a big sigh of thick late afternoon summer air before he started talking. He looked his most out of place in the charm and wonder of a Chicago summer—that severe face was winter all over, Ray decided, and only a big coat with big 1980s-style pads could hide his lack of shoulders. It didn't bother Ray though; Noah was still good company.

"So Tracy's gone and you're free at last."

"Yes. This is going to be such a nice summer. Ever notice you like a place best right before you leave it?"

"I haven't left a lot of places before now."

"It's the opposite with people though, I get sick of people."

"No, leaving people is the worst, there's no guarantee you'll ever see them again. You can always come back to a place."

"Unless a storm destroys it, or a fire."

Noah frowned. "The weather would still be the same."

"Nuclear winter."

Noah coughed, and almost managed to laugh. "Okay then, I guess I will miss Chicago after it's bombed."

"I sure won't miss Tracy. I hope she gets hit by a bus on her way home."

"Isn't that a little extreme?"

"Doesn't feel that way to me. Didn't you hate your nanny or whatever you had?"

"My au pair."

"Oh right, because she was French, right?"

"German. Most languages just use the French term."

"Oh my God, no one cares."

Noah sighed. He cared.

"I don't know, the stuff with Nadine got weird at the end. I was getting too old, and something was up with her and my older brother, I sort of caught on to that later, something sexual."

"You didn't have a molester nanny did you? Because then I'll wish for her to get hit by a bus instead. I'll do that for you."

"Not me, not as far as I remember it, but Mike and Sam are both better looking than me though, so . . . there's that to consider."

Ray laughed, extricated their hooch, and handed the squeeze bottle to Noah. "That was funny."

"Yeah, hilarious; always the witness and never the victim. So what do you have planned for this sentimental summer?"

"Oh, I've got ideas," Ray said as they began cutting through grass, heading towards the middle, the leafiest part of the park.

Smashing car windows, once he'd done it about three times, had completely lost its thrill. The last time, he was so without fear that he rooted through the car a bit and took what he could find: a phone charger, a bottle of hand sanitizer, and a key chain shaped like the Eiffel Tower. He was a tiny bit amused when he washed his hands of the crime using the hand sanitizer (before chucking it all in a trash can), but he had outgrown this pursuit, his skills had surpassed his task, and he was bored again.

Stealing was the next logical extension: not just breaking, but taking, gaining personally from what he was able to get away with doing to others. He had already started in small ways, stealing money from his mother's purse, stealing candy from his brother's bedside supply, but that was just to loosen up; he wouldn't really be testing himself until he started to steal from people who had no reason to trust him.

"What do you think about pick-pocketing?" Ray asked.

"I actually saw an article about how it's a dying art, nobody really carries around cash anymore, and credit cards get you caught too quickly, there are cameras in every store and ATM, there's a tech trail. You could steal phones, but people usually have them glued to their palms, they notice too quickly. If that's your plan for the summer, it's not great." Noah finished his downer's speech with a gulp of wine and a sour face.

"I was just trying to introduce my idea rhetorically. I think I might try stealing, but I already know what a pain it is. I wanted you to brainstorm with me, not just deliver a lecture, professor."

The wine was warm and already tasted like plastic that had been through a dishwasher. Ray made a face too.

"If you say so. But if you can't steal money and you can't sell what you steal, what's the point?"

"The thrill of the hunt, the joy of the sport! Why does anyone ever play a game of baseball if there's no trophy? They like it."

"I hate sports."

"I know you do."

QUEER
DUCKS

1

RAY'S SUMMER STARTED LATE, HE felt, because he wasted the first couple of weeks doing nothing. Literally nothing; full days spent with no one thing to say when asked, "So what did you do today?" He called or visited Noah, and Noah was always doing something, and that was what he told his family at the end of each day: "Nothing much, just relaxing, talked to a friend of mine who's recording bird sightings for an article." Then he would repeat some-to-all of Noah's prattle about classification, documentation, categorization, and people would still be impressed even though Ray had done nothing. Noah's life was so structured that it erected a kind of scaffolding around Ray's mere existence. That was a considerable power.

Eventually his parents came to know Noah by name. Ray would say, "a friend of mine," and they would ask, "Is that Noah?" It got to the point where his mother insisted to meet this boy, insisted so hard Ray wondered if she thought he was made up. He thought it was funny that after all of the lies he told, the actual truth sounded false to her. He'd have to lie to be believed forever, he decided.

Ray also got serious about his work after a fortnight of loafing, but it wasn't work he could crow about.

He started stealing for real, not just borrowing-without-asking sort of stealing from friends and family, but robbing items from stores. He was too young to steal anything he could use—he was eyeballed when he wandered near male accessories like wallets, cufflinks, watches, etc., but if he was browsing through the women's section of a store and wasn't approached by a sales chick beaming that *for your mom or your girlfriend?* face, he had a neat little trick for taking anything off a rack's peg. His secret? Long, opaque sleeves. It would be an easier grift in winter with sleeves and a coat on, but then stores know to be suspicious of a bulky coat, so maybe he was as favored by fate as ever.

All he had to do was pick up the front item of a display row: a bracelet, some hair pins, jangly useless key chains, earring bobbles . . . and let the second item on the row slip between his skin and his sleeve. He would pull off the first thing, let the second one sink to his elbow, then put the first one back like it just wasn't the right look. There aren't security tags on cheap costume danglers, so by the end of June he had a creepy hoard of lady's jewelry in an unused recipe box on his windowsill. He didn't fondle his treasure much, but he did like to sit at his telescope and stroke the box. He was quite fond of what its contents meant about his potential.

Boredom naturally set in though; stealing isn't the end, it's the means to something greater, the same way money isn't the thing to want, it's the way to acquire what you want. He began to give away the jewelry as gifts, first to girls in his periphery. Flirting with them became easier than ever, he could capture their whole attention with the right little gift and presentation ("I saw the color and thought of your eyes/hair/hands," whatever). It granted him so much good will and devotion that he started gifting things to his mother, even searching for bits and bobs she might actually like, which is a terrible thing for a criminal to do, act with a consistent motivation. But this phase of his development was short-lived, because Mother was a bitch about every gift.

"What is this for? What did you do that you're trying to distract me from?"

"Where are you getting the money for this stuff? I mean it's cheap, but it's not free, I hope you're not spending your allowance on this type of stuff."

"Raymond, do I look like I can't pick out my own jewelry? Your father can't even guess at my preferred settings, and he's been trying for years, just stop. It's nice that you're thinking of your old mother, but please . . . just stop."

So after a series of rebuffs like those, Ray started giving his gifts to Noah's mother, and she actually appreciated it.

"Oh, how sweet of you!" Faye cooed at the first one, a necklace Ray laced into his fingers like a cat's cradle web, with a heavy, quarter-sized clock locket hanging in the middle; a dense little egg in a nest. "Oooohhh, look at that! I love little charms like this."

The locket's cover had a pair of lovebirds on a branch etched into the filigree—Ray snagged it because it reminded him of Noah, and he thought the boy might like to see such an ornament nestled in his mother's bosom. Ray bestowed the chain over Faye's head like some royal raiment of mink and trinkets. She gave him a true mother's smile for doing that, the kind Noah must have seen all the time growing up. Ray had never been the target of one before, and it made his thieving habit feel not just fun and challenging, but right: the correct choice to have made.

By the summer solstice, Ray finally couldn't keep his work from Noah for another moment. Once Noah asked his mother about that locket, it was time to pay back all of Noah's stuffy lectures with his own passion and purpose.

"Did you steal a necklace from your mom and give it to mine?" That's how Noah brought it up. He wasn't angry about it; he asked it contemplatively, like he'd been trying to deduce the origin of that locket as a puzzle since he first spotted it.

"No," Ray told him, his face blank, his speech uninflected and honest. "I stole it from a fake boutique in the hipster part of town." Ray kicked off his shoes as he said this, pulling his legs onto Noah's bed and crossing them shin-over-shin in a meditation pose.

"Really?" Noah asked, leaning back in his desk chair, striking his psychiatrist's pose, and picking up a pen just to set it stately against the corner of his mouth. "Go on," he said.

And Ray did. He lied to Noah like he lied to everyone, about his habits with girls, about his grades, about his evenings alone, and Noah knew better than to believe him (unlike every other idiot Ray knew), and yet still Noah liked him, or at least found him fascinating. So about his work, Ray decided to tell the truth, finally.

And when the reality of Ray also kept Noah fascinated, that's when Ray really started to like him.

2

NOAH'S SUMMER WORK HAD MOSTLY been as serious as Ray and his audiences believed.

Number one: he never left his education and exploration on the subject birds; he always had one book open, one trip planned, one paper started, or more cataloging to do.

Number two: law isn't a subject one can just wing; with his decision made to follow Ray to the University of Michigan, Noah pulled up the last decade of course schedules, downloaded their syllabi, and started compiling a list of cornerstone textbooks to read before he even arrived on campus.

Number three: college isn't just an expensive book club; Noah looked up every professor he'd have access to, searched their accomplishments and standings, and picked those he wanted to ingratiate himself with in the hopes of having them as future references. That would mean taking any class they happened to teach, lurking near them for any opportunities to aid their work, and never correcting some pet opinion they uselessly advocated, no matter how wrong Noah might know them to be. He was willing to make that nearly insufferable sacrifice of his own principles, that's how much Noah demanded success in his pursuit of a law degree.

But his oddest study, his secret study, was the one he had taken up on the subject of Raymond Klein. He'd found Ray a curiosity since that Halloween when the boy charmed his mother, but Ray's behavior during this happy, hopeful summer was captivating. First of all, Noah wasn't so drunk the night of his birthday that he didn't remember that hooligan habit of Ray's the next day, how he worked at trying to smash into cars like some slum kid. Moreover, Noah knew the majority of everything Ray said was a lie (not out of disrespect, but out of a distasteful habit) . . . except for his tall tales of crime. They were still fictions—Noah never believed Ray had ever mugged or assaulted anyone (not yet anyway), and besides: whose birding gun had he used to fire a hole through an old jacket so he could tell idiotic people he'd been shot at by thugs? Who could get swept up in a play when they'd helped build the set and seen the rehearsal? No, Noah knew none of that talk was *true*, but . . .

Noah had seen that Ray could pretend to be enchanting, that's what made Faye like him so much, that any young man would bother to impress her when she was slumped and frumpy at home. But Ray's eyes became glassy doll eyes for that act; it wasn't his true sentiment. However, when Ray told lies about crime, his eyes ignited—that glassy sheen became molten and he stopped using body language to communicate and started gesticulating with his hands. They blossomed into explosions of action, they pointed as guns, they shaped around his face to describe the emotions he never felt, but imagined intensely.

No, the desire Ray had for those particular fantasies was not a lie, and his occasionless 'gift' to Faye confirmed it.

Noah had been taking a break to mull his latest section of Nietzsche anyway, so he'd started investigating Ray's behavior in psychology texts: compulsive lying, surface charm coupled with good looks, criminal tendencies . . . if Ray were more interested in sex he'd be a new Ted Bundy, but any time Ray slung lies about sex, he was cold, external, outside of his body in the way he talked about motions instead of emotions. He certainly found theft much more arousing than girls, and besides that: Noah always recognized another virgin when they tried to fib about sex. The initiated always admitted to awkwardness, uncomfortable fits, ripe smells, bad timing . . . apparently the sex left them prouder than all of that indignity; virgins never had anything embarrassing to say—their humiliation was already too great to compound.

The habitual lying led Noah into all sorts of mental subgenres, to addicts, narcissists, Munchausen hosts, schizophrenics . . . all of it too severe to apply to Ray. Ray lied for a simple reason: because he'd been brought up by a strict, know-it-all nanny. And, just when he was about to outgrow her, he made a strict, know-it-all friend in Noah. He was a bit of a self-saboteur, but he lied like a future politician or lawyer, no worse than that. Noah was even envious sometimes— Ray could be a jury lawyer if he wanted to be, Noah never even considered it. He lacked the raw talent it takes to lie to most people so convincingly.

"That's new," he said of his mother's deep-chained locket when he noticed it after Ray left the house that day. Faye had left it on all afternoon over her body-dampened pajama top, probably to feel a little smartened up and pretty.

"Ray gave me this, isn't that sweet? He said he saw this and thought of me, but look at the birds," she said, holding the locket out towards Noah but not removing it from her neck. "He obviously thought of you when he saw it, but you're too dour to wear jewelry." She was joking. She was happy.

Noah smiled at her, but it wasn't a real smile. He was a touch jealous, but also suspicious of more lies. Was that something of Ray's mother's? His grandmother's? Some stuffy aunt's who liked Victorian-looking knickknacks?

"Look, the clock runs and everything," Faye said, snapping the cover open and showing Noah a very new and modern little watch. So it wasn't an heirloom or overly valuable; would anyone in his wealthy family keep something so common, fake, and cheap in their house? Was this some junk re-gift that Ray appropriated because birds always brought the name Kaplan to his mind these days?

Noah told Faye that the necklace highlighted her elegance, then he brooded until he next saw Ray, wondering just what the introduction of a clock locket was all about.

"Did you steal a necklace from your mom and give it to mine?" he asked Ray bluntly the very next time his friend waltzed unannounced into Noah's room.

"No, I stole it from a fake boutique in the hipster part of town," and that brought Noah back from the brink of suspicion—it was Ray's urge for crime again, and he was developing. Noah had the scientist's sweetest opportunity: to watch a specimen evolve.

"Really?" Noah asked, channeling all the psychiatrist characters he had seen in movies, probably badly acting inaccurate vanity-driven storytelling, but it worked. "Go on," he said, and Ray did, as if he had been waiting for Noah to pop that question all summer.

Though Noah had been irreligious since he realized how his own birth had made his mother sick, he puffed a small sigh of gratitude—a faithful sort of thanks aimed high in the sky—that he had finally said the right thing.

3

RAY TOLD NOAH ALL ABOUT his thieving, but mostly the way someone comfortably confesses all their college mistakes in an end-of-life autobiography—he was done stealing. At least, he was done with the lifting of silly jewelry, and he didn't sense the glimmer of glamour when he imagined big time thefts anymore. When he first started lifting bracelets, he didn't see them as glittered plastic, he saw them as tennis diamonds, and when he walked to the train station from the store with something up his sleeve, he pretended he was shopping for which car he'd hotwire for a ride home. His inner critic (whose voice had begun sounding like Noah that summer) was hardly heard at the beginning; that's when theft was fun.

But once he got away with it over a dozen times, and the girls he knew started to be unimpressed by his 'gifts,' the inner critic was loud and relentless. *This is no real jewelry, but stealing it could still ruin your life if you're caught, and for what? Where's the gain? You can't hotwire cars anymore, not the new ones anyway—you'd have to hack the computers in them and you're useless with computers. Go home, Ray.* So he knocked it off. Maybe he'd return to stealing someday if a better opportunity presented itself, maybe he'd only gain a bit of light-handedness, no matter. Ray immediately moved on.

When he was disappointed and purposeless, Ray had a tendency to sink into a mire of dejection—he knew this about himself, though very few others did, not since he'd started keeping stashes of alcohol on hand to boost his cheer in emergencies. His family thought it was a childhood trait he'd outgrown. Ray just treated himself in secret.

With stealing suddenly commonplace and boring, Ray went back to the roots of his passion: his old detective novels. He tried getting Noah into these treasures, but it was like trying to force jazz on someone who didn't even like music, there was no entry port in his brain for the books Ray loved as a kid. Noah would read every one of them, but he analyzed them too much. He missed the point every time, but never for lack of trying. It was sad.

The last day Ray stole some mall stand crap, Ray came home to his novels and started tearing through them again, using an embroidered hair ribbon from the theft box as a bookmark. He got into crime because it gained the attention of manly, world-wise detectives like the ones he grew up reading, but . . . he started to ask himself when skimming lightly through his old Sherlock Holmes books again—why had he skipped over the idea of detecting? Holmes and Watson compare it to the thrill of committing crime all the time, except they have every right to do it! Holmes was congratulated, rewarded, awed, and all for understanding the warped mind of criminals way too well. It takes one to know one, doesn't it? That's how Ray got into his next hobby.

Sure, you can't just call yourself a PI and start following people—they'll still call you a stalker if you're caught at it—that's why Ray started following the bottom rungs of the city first. They had no power to snitch on him and much more interesting days than regular citizens. There was a beggar woman who frequented the train station near the University of Chicago, Ray's admissions counselor mentioned her. She was always digging through garbage and picking up things for her heaping shopping cart with the rickety wheel. Ray spent two days waiting for the last train just hoping she'd wander by, and when she finally did, he followed her on the rest of her day's journey.

He saw this hag through a strange route of alleys, watched her pull soda cans and clothes out of dumpsters and bins, and pile them into her cart. He wondered if there wasn't anything criminal she was up to—she'd make the perfect drug dealer or pick-up person; she was never hassled by cops unless she left the alleys or went for trash locked up on private property instead of free out on the street. He followed her for five days over a two-week period. She had a schedule and a regular route and he thought for sure when someone walked outside and put a heavy kid's backpack next to their trashcan that it was happening: the drug drop-off, the money pick-up: *what was it?* The thrill that raced through Ray as he struggled to keep his nonchalant about-to-light-a-smoke stance against the corner building was what he had wanted to find again, so it was already mission accomplished for him. But wouldn't it be great to be right in his suspicions too? Noah loved being right so damn much, there must be some extra joy in that.

But it turned out the backpack, which his hag lady certainly inspected, was full of puke residue and a tied baggy of bathroom trash—some kid in that house must have gotten sick of their homework, nothing special about that. Then the bag lady parked her cart, waddled into the narrow gap between two brick buildings, and squatted to pee just near where someone's central air intake tube stuck out. Ray watched her do it, but by the end of her stream he was thoroughly disenchanted with her. She was as dull as anyone else.

After that it was days before Ray saw someone new to tail—this guy was one of the crazy ranting types usually on Chicago transit, but today he was outside in the bright, happy summer day, wandering a busy street of theater and restaurant goers, with a runny stream of diarrhea streaked down one pant leg and leaking out over his shoe as he hobble-walked along. *That condition probably chafes*, Ray thought, circling upwind of him and pretending to check his phone so he could snap a picture and take notes of the guy's crazy spiel.

He almost texted the picture to Noah, but he knew what would happen if Noah found out he was shadowing vagrants: *Well, I bet a guy dripping in shit smells good*, followed by, *He might really be crazy as a jaybird—if he figures out you're following him around you might get knifed*, and eventually, *If you want to find criminals to follow, go page for some politician, this dude is just homeless and crazy, maybe on drugs or off meds, either one.*

And then Ray's interest was suddenly gone: just thinking through a Noah-style lecture had the same effect of hearing it; his project suddenly felt pointless again. He'd have argued with the real Noah for a little longer, tried to quote some of his favorite fictional detectives in support of the philosophy and dignity behind the profession, but he would have butchered the quotes, and Noah would have corrected him, and he'd have felt just as deflated as he did alone, except there'd be a witness to his defeat.

"Never leave a witness," Ray muttered, walking away from the poo-pants man in the direction of home and a daytime secret drink. He wanted to return to his life of crime already, but in what branch of it did he belong?

4

NOAH WAS EXPLAINING HIS VIEWS on Nietzsche's views on the fourth of July when the boys finally joined forces.

"Isn't that Superman philosophy the one Hitler used?"

Noah scoffed and rolled his eyes. "When Nietzsche spoke about a superior race, he meant the evolution of the whole human race, not the Aryans."

"If you say so, but you wouldn't be the first self-hating Jew in the world."

"I'm more Jewish than you are, your mother's a Catholic, so excuse me if I say your authority on Jewishness isn't exactly rabbinical, okay?"

"There, see, you just accused me of having inferior blood because of my racial lineage, that must be the Nietzsche talking."

Noah snorted and Ray laughed, and their giggles trailed off slowly; they were enjoying the twilight ending of an excellent repartee.

"No, the thing with Nietzsche is that he's speaking cerebrally about evolution, the kind of evolution that makes human attempts at religion void because we'd be reaching a state of actual spiritual being. We'd be seeing colors we don't even know are around us, understanding time the way it really is, and not this day/night/harvest season animalistic calculating we've been doing so far. But when you talk about the Übermensch, naturally the master-race idiots will try to glom onto your philosophy, thinking it props up a future of pasty blond people instead of a future of humans who are no longer locked into base, bodily concerns because they're finally beings of higher thought."

Ray had picked up one of Noah's Nietzsche books during this discourse. Noah had brought all his Nietzsche material downstairs to transcribe the quotes he needed and check their original German in case he disagreed with the translations he was using for an English-language essay he wanted to write—he was prepping a subject-specific paper draft for the law school applications in his near future.

Ray must have stopped listening the second he opened *Human, All Too Human*, because he started chortling the second he found a quote he wanted to read out loud to Noah.

"Nietzsche himself says that apparently his books 'contain snares and nets for short-sighted birds,' guess he's talking about you there, isn't he?"

Noah smiled without any happiness (he did not consider this facial expression a grimace, but everyone else did). "Actually he's talking about the contemporaries who say his books are dangerous to the impressionable. Nietzsche, of course, disagreed with what those people said. They couldn't grasp the concepts of metaphor or irony, they thought Nietzsche meant every word they saw in his books."

"If you say so," Ray told him. He'd come by Noah's house unannounced on this national independence holiday in blue shoes, red shorts, and a white polo shirt. Half Jewish or not, he looked like an American dream come to life.

Noah finished talking, mostly because he enjoyed the sound of his own voice, since Ray went to the window and gazed out at the bright, warm day.

"In that book's intro, Nietzsche also hopes that his philosophy would someday be understood by an evolved man: 'He looks gratefully back—grateful for his wandering, his self-exile and severity, his lookings afar and his bird flights in the heights.'" Noah liked that quote quite a bit, not just for the bird imagery, but because he himself was an ascetic, disciplined, lonely young man, and maybe someday he would look back on his current years with the knowledge that they were worthwhile, and in fact the only true path to his own happiness.

"It's too dry out," Ray speculated, squinting at the grass and trees on Noah's street. "Do you think the city will try to ban neighborhood fireworks tonight?"

"They can try," Noah said, "but morons are always going to want to light explosives."

Ray snorted. "There's that optimism everyone loves about you."

"Admit it, tonight would be a great night for an arsonist, the cops will be writing off every fire as some patriotic accident."

"Will they?" Ray came back with, first as a tease, but then he got quiet as he perched back on the couch. He was still looking outside. Noah sat with his back to the sunny day on purpose—a warm, cheery day is frivolous, distracting, and he had work to do.

"I bet setting a fire feels really powerful," Ray said. He bit his bottom lip. He was thinking hard.

"Don't want to be a thief anymore?" Noah asked him, this time without that attitude tone. He actually wanted to know the answer to this question, to get Ray talking on the couch again.

"I stopped stealing before I even told you about it," Ray said quietly, glancing about in case there were any eavesdroppers in a house that was empty of everyone except an upstairs, napping Faye. "Until last week I was stalking homeless people in case they were criminals, but outside of vagrancy and filth, I saw nothing very criminal about them. Now I'm thinking I should try something else. Do you think I'd like setting fires?"

"Hmm," Noah considered. "You like attention. Giving what you stole as gifts got it for you, and if you'd found a criminal you'd have gotten to report them, that was the fantasy, wasn't it? You can't take credit for setting fires."

"True." Ray cocked his head sharply, looking from window to window as if looking for targets. "Maybe it isn't attention I want, maybe it's just a big thing, like drama."

"A spectacle?"

"Yes! I want to set a fire tonight, you were right, this is the perfect night for it." His eyes had their own fire back, the boy was on the verge of an internal ecstasy suddenly. It reminded Noah of another tenet of Nietzsche's philosophy, the goal to 'become what one is.' Ray throws himself into his pursuit with a recklessness Noah would never dare for himself, despite how hard and relentlessly he works to make himself the man he will become.

"Hmm," Noah said again, this time with a weak voice, a reflection of an insecurity or jealousy that he'd just found in comparing himself to Ray's purity of passion.

"You should come with me tonight," Ray said out of mercy.

And though an hour ago Noah would never have predicted this outcome, he said, "Okay."

5

Ray's Independence Day was coming along swimmingly. He thought that morning that he'd be in for another day of lemonade with old people on the back patio, expensive hot dogs that tasted just as slurry-meaty as the cheap ones, and listening to his mother complain: if the fireworks were cancelled she'd whine about how un-American that was; if the fireworks happened, she'd complain about the noise; if they were too far away to make noise, she'd say they were disappointing duds . . . she'd whine about something until every man in her life wanted to strangle her, and then they'd all take their rage to bed.

But thank his lucky stars and stripes, he had Noah. All that unbearable reading he endured really did fill the guy's head with thoughts—he came up with a perfect crime that Ray had never even brushed against, and it was the perfect night to execute it!

"I can't believe you're really coming out with me," Ray told him as they stood in their own homes, connected by a phone call, looking for all the domestic flammables they could find. Ray had already collected every match, lighter, and portable candle in the place. He was thinking of fuses now, or rags soaked in lighter fluid . . . how could he get a significant fire started without getting burned? Or caught?

Noah had an answer to this too.

"I saw a show about an arsonist once, you'll want to make a delayed incendiary device, something that burns slowly and then ignites something flammable so you have time to leave the scene."

"Incendiary," Ray said, pausing mid-reach for the emergency snowstorm lantern (he was thinking of burning oil, even though somewhere in his mind he knew it was electric). "I really like that word."

"We shouldn't be saying any of this over the phone, it's probably being recorded by something."

Ray laughed and left the pantry, the lantern discarded from his mind and forgotten. "Paranoid about the government?"

"Or about some nanny device on your cell phone. You know your mother is the type to record all your conversations if she could."

"You overestimate her interest in me. Now that I'm leaving, it's like I'm a lodger who didn't renew his lease, like she's waiting for a stranger to leave already."

"No wonder you like my mom so much."

They met up on the sidewalk between their houses and headed for the nearest bus stop. Ray's idea was to find a crappier but still mostly white part of town so they wouldn't stand out. They needed to find something to light up: a shed, a dumpster, a garage, hopefully something still made out of wood.

Ray got more excited as their bus carried them further north, his foot tapping a dance tune on the floor and his hands playing with a cigarette because he thought that might be a good incendiary whatever, what Noah said. He'd gotten the pack of cigarettes during his stealing phase, a half-empty pack someone had set next to him on a bench, which Ray picked up under his backpack when he stood to leave. He kept them because he thought smoking might make a nice habit (certainly one that would incense his mother), but now they could be used for something really special.

Noah was feeling their approach to this mission too, the way he started wiping sweat from his forehead and then setting it on the back of his hand, and the way his eyes started swirling like he felt dizzy.

"Calm down," Ray told him. "You're with me, and nothing bad ever happens to me."

"That's true," Noah said, whimper-coughing without humor. It really was.

They failed at their first attempts: one in the unkempt brush of a vacant lot, one in the trellis of some abandoned, boarded up, ramshackle house. Ray wanted to stay and watch to see if the flame caught, but Noah was boss in one area: he insisted that Ray light the cigarette, or the wrap of matches, and drop it and walk away.

"Walk around the block and circle back to see if it worked, don't be so stupid so early."

Ray was in a grand enough mood that he didn't even mind Noah getting snippy with him; Noah had low nerve, but plenty of brainpower. Compared to him, Ray really might seem stupid sometimes, but Noah was an exception unto himself.

Ray finally got so insistent on seeing some soaring flames that he had Noah dowse an old sock with lighter fluid, and Ray threw a match onto that in the corner of some Porta-Potty on a bare-bones construction site. It might have been a demolition site for all Ray could see—no one was building in this area, but certainly the city still tore shit down.

That plan finally worked.

They saw the flames spark and start licking at the plastic of the outhouse, blacking and melting it. Noah insisted they walk a full four-block circle before they returned, because he insisted they only walk past once to avoid suspicion in case there was a crowd.

And there was a crowd. Or at least there were a few spectators who'd stepped out of their lives and into Ray's to look at what he'd done. They were trying to find a long hose or a bucket to keep the fire from spreading away from the shitter. They were speculating about how the disaster had started.

The heat and color of the fire did nothing to excite Ray, but he wasn't disappointed, because he immediately inserted himself into the neighborhood's conversation.

"Must be some fireworks accident," he declared as they approached. Noah stiffened but did nothing to scold Ray.

"Nobody's wasting money on fireworks around here, this is some asshole smoking in the john." This was told with tired authority by a man wearing a cleaner's uniform, clearly headed to or from his crappy job.

"Maybe it's a prank," Ray said. "You know, teenagers or kids or something."

"I guess you would know that," said an old lady who seemed too tired to even say this, and turned back to her house halfway through the sentence with a slow, creaking walk. She couldn't find a hose or schlep water, so there was no reason to stand around watching.

"It's nothing big," said the first guy to another neighbor. "Can you handle this, Phil? I can't be late."

Phil nodded, they both agreed that no one would even have to call the fire department, and the rest of the two or three lookie-loos dispersed. Noah started leaving too, and Ray had to follow him, feeling a little dejected that he hadn't caused more of a panic, but then this was only his first attempt, so it would only get better . . . right?

"I'm not doing that ever again," Noah told him firmly the second they were far enough away to not be heard.

"Yeah," Ray said. He probably wouldn't either—it was too much trouble for too little reaction, and without Noah's help or acknowledgement . . . what was the point?

6

IF RAY THOUGHT HIS EXPERIENCE with crime was disappointing (and he did, and he made it very clear with his deflated attitude every other week), he would be emotionally felled if he experienced it all the way Noah did. Noah had never been afraid of hard work or lengthy mental endurance or even public speaking, but his forays into bad behavior with Ray gave him sickening feelings of anxiety and paranoia. If Ray thought about his own parents finding out any of his misdeeds, he smirked. He would say something like, "It would serve them right, I'm not the one who raised me so terribly." But just the thought of having to answer for that sort of idiocy to Faye made Noah want to injure himself. He'd considered himself a skeptic and at least a Nietzschean sort of atheist for years, but committing petty crimes made him understand the severe mortal guilt that made religious enthusiasts flagellate themselves in the hopes of making up for their many moral deficiencies. Noah would put himself through a lot of physical torment before he'd tell his mother he'd set a shed on fire in a poorer neighborhood just to watch Ray watch it burn. He couldn't stand the thought of disappointing her, not after all she still endured for bringing him to life in the first place.

So why risk it?

On the way home from the shed fire, Noah made himself a resolution. He was sitting under the bleak lights of a public bus, surrounded by incredibly average, noddingly tired, dumpy Midwesterners, and he was sitting next to Raymond Klein who, even in his sort of post-coital come-down from their tepid little arson, out-shown the whole city. The way Ray couldn't stop chasing crime no matter how often it didn't dazzle him . . . that is how Noah stuck with Ray. It couldn't just be his handsome face, because Noah found a lot of good-looking people vile. It couldn't just be his smarts, because he wasn't that smart, and he certainly never worked hard enough to live up to his potential. And it couldn't be just because he liked Noah so much . . . could it? There wasn't enough data to know the answer to that question; the sample size of those who liked Noah was incredibly small.

Ray could be a bit of a user. Noah knew that, and knew that he liked being used by Ray because it netted him more time in the boy's presence. He was under the impression however that their friendship was as unique in Ray's life as it was in his own, and he knew a way to test that hypothesis. He spent the bus ride sweating even though a cold vent was blasting right into his left armpit as he rested his forearm against the windowsill. He was trying to gin himself up for an act even risker than setting that fire.

"I said I wouldn't do that again," Noah began when they disembarked and started walking home through the summer haze of the air in their neighborhood—it was a rather sweet sort of miasma here, in streets full of trees and flowers, much better than the junkyard where they melted that shithouse.

"Yeah, I heard what you said, I won't bother you about it anymore," Ray snapped in response.

Noah waited a beat before continuing, until Ray realized that he'd interrupted after just the beginning of a sentence and looked at Noah, waiting for the rest.

"I might consider doing more with you, because I know it matters to you, and honestly you need a little more caution in that department, you need contingency plans and you never think those out in advance."

"Okay," Ray said. He was excited. He'd take criticism like a perfect gentleman if he knew it was part of a compliment sandwich; he wanted that middle part more than he wanted to argue.

The problem was, Noah didn't know how to say the next part. What he wanted . . . it wasn't sex, but it was still going to feel like asking for it, like dealing for it, like prostitution. He thought (unhelpfully) of the mating rituals of birds, about all the literal puffing and calling and flaunting and strutting they did for love; there's nothing subtle about their declarations of desire for their mates. But as a human: there was no rival to peck at, no color on Noah's breast, and no nest full of stolen shiny things that could make this statement for him. He had to find the courage to use words, and they wouldn't be the best words for it either—English was no lover's tongue compared to so many others he knew.

"What are you getting at?" Ray asked, still happy, still smiling, cajoling Noah because he was about to get what he wanted, he was just waiting to hear the price of it.

"I, guh . . ." Noah believes he said, before he looked over Ray's physique trying to figure out how to phrase it. He didn't want a gay boyfriend to bring home to mom, and he didn't want a brainless make-out session, and he wasn't comfortable enough with his own body to want it being touched too much, but looking at Ray . . . he just wanted *more*. What amount of crime would make Ray lose his taste for it? How much heroin was too much for a junkie? When would enough time pass to let Noah get over Ray? Some people could find rock bottom, hit it, and bounce; other people were limitless.

"You're limitless, and I wish you would, like . . ." Noah gestured weakly at Ray. Did he mean touch? Touch me, let me touch you? Fuck.

Ray raised his eyebrows, but he didn't look away in disgust.

"This is an exchange, right? Like a fair trade? My hobbies for what you want?"

It didn't sound very special when it was put that way, but, "Yeah," Noah said.

Ray nodded, and he looked around their separation corner to make sure no one was watching them, and pulled Noah into a huge hug; a hug that lifted Noah off his feet, and then his feet off the ground.

"Yeah," was all Ray said in agreement, but the way he looked directly into Noah's eyes, nodding in earnest, it was clear that they had a deal.

7

AUGUST WAS RAY'S LAST MONTH IN Chicago before the move to the University of Michigan. He would have that journey to himself—scheduling with Noah's transfer meant he wouldn't follow Ray for a week or more, which wasn't the sundering for Ray that it was for Noah. Would he miss having his partner in crime for a little while? Yes, but he could scout, and plan, and wait. Noah's interest in Ray, however, was much more vital, more . . . pressing. He was a very strange bird indeed.

Ray knew what Noah wanted was boyfriend stuff, maybe some sex stuff, in exchange for continuing to join in Ray's crimes. The idea bothered Ray less than he would have guessed, especially if it meant he didn't have to go through the existential shit-show of giving up his passion, or the one-man audience he had for it. Ray didn't have to like it, he just had to let it happen to him, and if Noah wanted reciprocation . . . well, they would just have to negotiate that stuff in the fine print of their agreement.

But what Noah wanted wasn't that unpleasant. The handful of nights Ray took Noah out scouting for the houses that were summer homes (and thus robbable during the winter months), ended in the back seat with Ray drinking from his flask (for anesthetic purposes), then pretending to be drunker than he was. Then he let Noah touch him (over the clothes) or kiss him (not on the mouth) or grind against him, which is what Noah seemed to want. He wanted permission with a living doll for something the French call 'frottage'—Ray looked it up out of curiosity after the first odd night in his back seat, and he remembered the word in case he and Noah ever fought, since it'd be a good word to throw in his face. Ray had to be careful not to accidentally say 'fromage' if that ever happened, just like he had to be careful whenever saying either Napoleon or Neapolitan; languages were Noah's skill, not Ray's, and he certainly didn't want to embarrass himself.

Noah helped him pack for Michigan, and Noah spent the last day before his departure to the Great Lake State hovering near Ray like a restless ghost. Ray started to get a little annoyed as the day wore on—this was a moment of independence for him, the first real solo departure of his life, and having his buddy around was ruining it. Ray needed a quiet balcony and a sunrise vista and some dignified silence, not help loading his car.

"You know, absence makes the heart grow fonder," Ray said when he finally wanted Noah to say goodnight. They were at last done with the going-away dinner his parents were obligated to present, and done double-checking the schedule and alarms, and done separating the things that would stay from the things that would go. There was nothing left for Noah to 'help' with, and Ray had to be up early the next day, well rested for his long drive. It was time to part ways. "We're about to live in the same cement cell for a year, you should really start missing me now, you know? Before we start fighting over how to hang toilet paper on the roll or whatever."

"I already miss you. Michigan doesn't feel real to me at all," Noah whined. "I don't believe I'm actually going. You seem like you're already there."

"I wish," Ray said, with a little more earnestness than he meant to let out. "I'm sick of this house."

Noah looked around at the tastefully decorated walls, like Ray meant the house itself and not the home inside of it that had held him captive all his life. His bedroom, where Ray sat on his bed and Noah sat at the desk chair, was half-stripped. The only things left on the walls were things Ray considered belonging to his parents and not himself; the drawers were all empty, the closet only full of uncomfortable season-specific clothes. It looked like a guest room now, and it would be in a mere matter of hours, and Ray could hardly wait for that to happen.

"I worry that it's something I'll regret someday," Noah said, his eyes still roving the room. "A move this big can change the course of a life, or of a career."

Ray puffed out a huge sigh. "That's more deep than I'm thinking about it, I just want something new to happen to me. You can always come back if it's not right for you, and think of how nice that'll be, knowing for sure what was out there before you chose to stay in your hometown like a loser."

That got Noah to crack a sad smile, and at that opening Ray stood and patted Noah's shoulder to get him moving.

"At least our hometown is a world-famous city, not some cow pasture place without any stoplights," Noah said as he moved towards the door, down the hallway, closer and closer to the exit.

"There's that sunny side of you, that's a nice note to leave on," Ray said, almost pushing Noah out the door with the hand he never took off his shoulder, just to keep him from stalling or loitering. Noah touched that hand with his own as he faced the darkness outside, and stepped out from under Ray's palm with nothing but a scoffing, sniffling sort of noise—Ray couldn't tell for sure because Noah had already turned away from him. He didn't look back as he walked down the front walk of the Klein home either.

"I bet there are better cities than this one out there," Ray called after Noah with a brief lick of sympathy he almost never felt. "We'll find them together, as soon as you join me!"

Noah held up his hand in acknowledgement of Ray's words, and kept on walking home.

8

NOAH FELT A LOOMING SENSE of sabotage as he prepared to follow Ray to the University of Michigan. He really couldn't undo it—payments were made, paperwork was submitted, bags were packed—but it still felt impossible. How could he really leave home to live in some crusty Michigan dorm? No more dinners with Mom, no more quiet hours of study in his comfortable bedroom, and a whole new schedule to adjust to? But right when he was about to abandon the whole transfer regardless of the cost, there was Ray to consider. Chicago without Ray? Death by tedium. And Michigan with Ray? An adventure.

They'd live together, they'd be transplants together, a team. Ray could never find a closer friend than the one who'd left home for him. They'd go forth to classes each morning with inside jokes, with each other's secrets . . . they'd be more thoroughly bonded. People keep their college friends for life, no other relationship could touch that.

So Noah said goodbye to Ray and promised himself that they would only spend a week apart; that's what made him get through it without any whining or blubbing. He was being the most dramatic of everyone involved with the change. Even Ray's parents didn't linger over him as much as Noah did, and this was the flight of their own baby nestling. But then, Noah judged them against his own mother, who looked wound up with worry every time he saw her in the days before he left.

"I'm sorry," he finally blurted to her after she turned off the TV for the night, on his last night at home. Noah had collected a packet of transcripts and a stack of recommendation letters from one of his professors that day, and there was nothing left between him and Ray but the drive.

"Hi, Sorry, nice to meet you, I'm Faye," was her response. She was smiling, but her face drooped around it. Noah didn't say anything until she broke the quiet spell her sad joke had conjured. "Don't be sorry for me. It's my job to feel sorry for me, but I feel happy for you," she told him.

Noah nodded, even though he didn't believe her. "Okay," he said.

"You're going to be so happy once you get there, all this sorry stuff will go away, trust me." And that, she was actually right about.

The drive to Michigan was a numbness. It was four pure hours of near-silence, with nothing but the hum of the tires on the road for Noah to hear. He couldn't stand the thought of having the radio on, of listening to idiotic pop songs and crass advertisements on such a momentous occasion. Instead he let his accelerator foot madden him with its tension, and he let his worries and fantasies repeatedly stomp through his head. Surely Ray would get sick of him when they actually shared a room, or maybe he'd already realized how much he enjoyed Noah's absence after just one week alone. Noah let the thoughts repeat without fighting them. He was ready to turn right around and drive home if his pessimism all came horribly true.

He parked first near the visitor's center, then again near the admission's office, and for the last time where he actually belonged, in his own dorm's lot. He left his car, full of his books and clothes and technology and vitals, so he could locate his and Ray's room and see if he should even bother to unpack.

Noah spent almost a full minute fitting his key in the lock quietly before gently turning the handle. He wanted to keep his presence secret for as long as possible. He was right in this urge, because he managed to step inside without waking up a passed-out Ray, still sleeping with his socks and belt and watch on, and with a breath that stank of alcohol when Noah crouched down to be on level with his friend's face. There was sweat on Ray's upper lip, and drool resting beneath his slightly parted mouth, and the hair that was usually combed back perfectly, nearly compulsively over each ear, was that morning matted greasily on his forehead. And still he looked good to Noah.

Noah wanted to stroke the hair back into place, but instead he pushed Ray's shoulder with the palm of his hand, shifting him out of sleep.

"I guess you're not helping me with move-in," Noah said, surprised at how little it actually bothered him. It would be more fair after packing Ray up himself that Ray should pay him back with some unpacking, but he was just happy to find Ray so disheveled, so off-guard. That made him feel more on par with his buddy again, especially after all his concern that Ray might have magically outgrown him in just a week away at college.

"Yugg," or a noise that sounded like that, was all Ray had to say for himself. He put one hand over his own eyes and forehead, probably resisting the bright summer day blasting in through their one drapeless window. He put his other hand over Noah's whole face, weakly trying to block him out too, to cram him away, but there was no real push in that movement.

Noah smiled, and all the worry and tension that had delivered him to Michigan disappeared.

He had known it on some level all along: Ray wanted him here.

9

RAY WOULDN'T CHARACTERIZE HIMSELF AS a heartless person, but he knew what he was feeling as that first semester in Michigan progressed, and he knew what he was doing to deal with it; he was peeling away from Noah, and he was setting up escape hatches all over campus, ready for the first open window from which he could take flight.

Noah stayed the same. That isn't a bad thing, having a true core self that never changes. People who don't pretend to be someone they're not, not even in college, have a certain dignity that can't be denied (though they're probably duds at parties). But everyone else went to college to explore themselves, to find out what they were capable of, and that's what Ray liked about college. Ray took this new stage as an opportunity to perform, and far from being an effective straight man, Noah was more like a pro wrestling heel, a saboteur.

"That's not the way it happened," Noah would say bluntly whenever Ray tried to embellish any of his crimes for an audience. He'd pop his big eyes halfway out of his head, searching for an answer he should have already had. He had no sense of art, this kid, no craftsmanship when it came to words, and he knew so many more words than everyone else put together! That knowledge was practically wasted on Noah.

He was scaring the civilians away from Ray, all the normal students attending the U of M fresh out of their hometown high schools. They thirsted for stories of Chicago, for someone bright and bold like Ray. Who doesn't love a cheerful criminal? History and politics are full of them! Fame or infamy, it didn't matter, everyone had the same quality of legacy, but Noah didn't think of the big picture in that way. Noah was Watson to Ray's Holmes, a horribly literal magician's assistant who revealed the mechanism behind every trick. He plotted the course of his life, and he was right about having the talent for details and contingency plans that Ray lacked, but what good is all that work and effort if it couldn't net him any attention?

Ray lived with Noah well (Noah was neat, but not yet a nag about it), and he still enjoyed Noah's company, their talks. Every week they managed to have a friend-to-friend debriefing about campus life: the sad qualifications of some of the adjunct professors, the sexual exploits of the TAs and the tenured (those tiers were the most lascivious in all of college), or the mental density and sluggishness of their so-called peers.

"Can you believe these people are all older than us? They're such *children*." Noah was particularly amazed now that no one knew he was still an infant babe; everyone here assumed he was a young-looking freshman, no one knew he ought to be in junior year of high school (same as Ray), and was instead a top-grade sophomore in college (unlike Ray).

"So many of them don't even do the reading for class, let alone read for pleasure," Ray agreed. "I'm surprised they get their shoes on the right feet every day."

"Oh, you've met some in shoes? I've seen so many walking around with filthy bare feet, I'm almost worried about their toes come winter."

Ray snorted, found his sip of soda leaking painfully out his nose, and no one else in his life had ever made Ray laugh like that. Noah was still his best friend.

And yet: who says you should live with your best friend?

The true intention to move started with Joey, a guy who would eventually go by Joseph like his parents wanted him to, and with a job and a wife they approved of, but in college he was still going by Joey like a boy. This guy liked the idea of Ray, liked to talk to him about moving to Chicago when Ray knew Joey's family had filled out and submitted his college applications for him. He didn't have the personal motivation to do anything he wasn't told to do, and even Ray couldn't tell him to try living in Chicago; a novice thief like Ray still considered Joey an easy mark. In fact, Ray once told him he looked like a Mark, though of course Joey didn't get the joke, even after it was explained to him. Noah thought it was funny.

Joey asked if Ray knew where he was rooming next year, did he want to get a four room suite-style dorm with Joey and his friends, because they were looking for their fourth. The reason for this: Joey's roommate was moving into a frat house the next year. A fraternity intrigued Ray, he had vaguely considered that option because his father was in a frat and would like to have his son join one too. When it occurred to him again, Ray realized that a frat might be the best way to put just one or two walls between him and Noah, and still keep him as a friend.

Ray turned down Joey, and Joey was actually pretty sore about it, because he's the one who started a rumor that Ray and Noah were gay together, that the rejection was all Ray's fault, his damage, his secrets. That added to the dissatisfaction Ray had for his living situation, because Noah didn't help put out that rumor at all. Their crime-for-coupling pact was suspended in Michigan, since they were both busy with classes, but Noah still tapped his shoulder instead of saying, "Hey, Ray," and Noah sat right next to him no matter how many chairs or how much bench was up for grabs, and Noah was jealous about people liking Ray too much—he'd had conversations with boys and girls alike that were basically him telling them, "You don't know Ray like I do."

It certainly didn't help that the only time Joey came by their dorm room looking for Ray was on one of the few instances that Ray and Noah woke up in the same bed together. With Ray's drinking, sometimes Noah would join him for the night without Ray noticing, or Ray would just land on the first bed he found and not care whose it was (and Noah certainly wouldn't correct him), and that was the story he tried to tell Joey when it was obvious that Ray had stumbled to answer the door from the same bed with a shirtless Noah in it: "I was so wasted, I must have fallen into the wrong bed by mistake when I passed out." But Joey didn't want to believe that bit of fabrication after he was turned down as a roommate, and that excuse certainly didn't explain why Noah would have stayed in the same narrow bed with a blacked-out Ray; Noah didn't drink that hard. People around campus were getting way too close to the truth about them, and so Ray started looking into frats.

Ray began wheeling and dealing until he could find a house that would let him move in without a year of pledging or hazing or whatever they do to the freshman. He wasn't a freshman, and he was capable of paying for the privilege of moving in early, or of replacing any undesirable member they had as soon as possible. It worked out for him: the Zeta Beta Tau house was on disciplinary suspension, they'd had to move their chapter off campus into a rented house, and they needed money as much as they needed well-behaved members. Why not the rich boy pegged to be the youngest person to ever graduate from the University of Michigan? That might just get ZBT off the Greek society shit list.

He was in.

All he had to do was break the news to Noah.

10

NOAH TOOK THE NEWS BADLY, but gradually.

He believed it when Ray said, "This isn't a me-and-you thing, this is a me getting serious thing." His sub-reasons: (1) a fraternity looked good to schools and employers, it makes a guy look like a friend and a joiner; (2) Noah was just *too fun*, Ray couldn't concentrate on his studies with his best friend right by his side; (3) his parents and his older brother were really pressuring him to get more of a social circle, "and you know why that is," Ray concluded with. Noah had sat quietly during the whole presentation, barely noticing how much the bright winter day outside made their little cell of a room look all the less impressive.

"Yeah," Noah said, "those rumors about us." They were becoming rumors about Noah more than Ray at this point, because Ray was out trying to combat them. He'd even gone to his older brother for advice on it, and the brother enlisted their parents in an anti-Noah campaign. Noah knew all about it, because he and Ray really were best friends, they didn't keep secrets from one another, except for this move-out idea. Ray already had it all set up, which means he'd been planning it for weeks, maybe since before the Christmas break. He couldn't even last one semester with Noah without looking for something better.

"Now don't start eyeing my side of the room yet," Ray said, switching from his bed to Noah's, where he could put his arm behind Noah's back and lean close to him, a half-gesture between stiffness and a hug. "They don't have a space open in the house until next year, and probably not until the Spring term, because they've got one of those loser fifth year seniors still trying to finish a thesis. He might be out sooner than Spring, but he can't stay any longer, so that's when I'll move. Plenty of time left for us."

Noah was convinced by Ray for months. The rest of their year was pleasant if hampered by Ray's new policy of chaperones, of never being seen alone in public together. Noah committed to another year in Michigan because at least it would begin with him and Ray living together, and in the semester it took to move Ray over to the ZBT house, Noah even tried to join a fraternity himself. He was very briskly rejected by them—those rumors about his sexuality were the most likely culprit—Noah was as unpopular as ever. It didn't bother him as long as he had Ray, but how long was that? A year passed between when Ray announced leaving and when he actually did it, but it felt like no time to Noah at all.

Ray's moving out coincided with a dangerous turn in Faye's health. Every day after his sixteenth birthday was a bad day for Noah.

The day Ray moved out all his new friends came into their room, cast judgmental eyes over Noah, over his overabundant books, and his wall of post-it notes in Sanskrit (to keep their contents secret from prying eyes), and Ray didn't even hug him goodbye, didn't even look at him, not in front the guys. He murmured, "See you around, dude," which is not something he'd ever called Noah before, and left his side of the room hideously stark and empty.

The day his father called Noah and told his son he *had* to come home during winter break, during every break, because they didn't know how much time Faye had left. Her kidneys were failing, she was going to dialysis, she was not high on the transplant list because she was too old and too weak, her body would just quickly wreck up a replacement organ that might save another person's young life, so she wasn't going to get one.

The day a blizzard hit and Noah was trapped in his single room alone for three days with nothing but an unapproved hotplate to keep him warm, knowing that Ray was in a large heated house drinking with his *brothers*.

The many, many days Ray was suspiciously too busy to hang out with Noah; couldn't grab dinner, see a movie, meet at some crowded event (Noah even offered to see sports if his piece of bleacher could be next to Ray's), but he always had plans to do something else. One day he even claimed he had to study, and that is when Noah felt truly and personally injured. That was a lie, and it was a sloppy one, and if Ray cared so little about Noah that he couldn't even make the effort to lie properly, then it really was his greatest fear come true: Noah left his mother in her final days for someone who left him in return. If he had any religion in him, Noah would have thought he was being justly punished. Instead, he did what Ray would have done: he stalked with the intention of ambushing his friend, so that at least the breakup would be formal.

Like Ray had once followed him through Chicago's snow with cheer and promises to get him to Michigan in the first place, Noah took after Ray's plumage in hopes of catching him alone.

Maybe Ray wasn't lying about being busy all the time, he really was surrounded at all hours of every day, in his room, in the dining hall, to and during and from every class. The way Noah finally got him alone was by being a terrible stalker. People noticed Noah's skulking, mentioned it to Ray, and because of that Ray detached from his acolytes and came to Noah on his own.

Noah left his room for a trip to a sandwich shop and a stop by his mail box, and on his way back to the dorm, Ray was suddenly in stride beside him, eating a sandwich from the same shop Noah had been at, with his own mail sticking out of his coat pocket. Noah couldn't stop his eyebrows from lifting in surprise. He was happy that Ray had snuck up on him so carefully, but he desperately hoped it didn't show on his face.

"Like the great detective, if you see no one, that is what you can expect to see when I follow you."

"What you *may* expect to see," Noah corrected him, "and I don't know why you always think you're Holmes and I'm Watson. I'm the weird, isolated, painfully smart one, you're the one with all the friends, who tells the best stories, because you're the best liar."

"Well, you're a terrible shadower like Watson, and you're clearly mad at me."

"What could I be mad at, I haven't seen you since you moved out."

"You've *seen* me, you've followed me." Ray was paying Noah back for correcting him.

"You know what I mean," Noah said, reaching the door to the room they once shared and getting his key out of his pocket.

"Got a new roommate yet?" Ray asked.

"Of course not," and with that answer Noah was pushed inside, and Ray pulled the key from the handle and locked them both inside.

"The way you're acting now is part of the reason we aren't roommates anymore. You're making this look like the falling out of a pair of cocksuckers."

"See, you said your reasons for leaving were all about you, not me. And I didn't invite you in. And we never did stuff like that."

"Why? Because you didn't want to? Or because you didn't have enough to trade for it yet?"

That made Noah quiet because he didn't exactly know the answer. In his silence, Ray came closer, and took everything they both still had in their hands, and moved all that stuff to the empty desk. He pulled Noah into a hug, and even kissed the side of his neck in apology.

"We're still friends," he told Noah, and Noah believed him. Again.

LIKE MINDS

1

Ray returns to Chicago after his Chernobyl semester, knowing that his lack of Noah was the main culprit. But how to win him back? There is a chance that Noah will still take Ray any way he can get him, but wouldn't that be pathetic on both their parts? Ray stripped of his sheen, picking up something he once threw away, and Noah too desperate to even care that he's a consolation prize? Surely one of them would find enough dignity to walk away if Ray makes this approach without care.

Ray goes into full courtship mode, the same way he does when he wants to convince a girl to hold his arm at a party. There are stages in this art, and it requires time. Ray plans to devote all of June to the process.

First up, a single rose, or since Noah's no usual conquest, a peacock feather that is also an inkwell pen. Noah likes birds, he wants to be a lawyer with fancy shit on his desk someday, that gift is literally two birds with one stone! Ray puts it in the Kaplan family mail box with a card that says, *Saw this and thought of you*, in his own handwriting, but without his name or signature. Noah will know who it's from.

The second salvo begins thusly: Ray finds out by talking with Mr. Kaplan that Noah visits his mother's grave with his aunt at least once a month (sometimes more often when he wants to go there alone). Mr. Kaplan is unaware of the boys' falling out, an assumption that Ray gambles on and is correct about (there are some things that no one will voluntarily tell their father). Ray stakes out the house early when Mr. Kaplan is on his way to work to get this information, and he pretends he is out jogging even though Ray never does any such thing. He stops, panting as if he's really out of breath after a slight run from the privacy wall, and he tells Mr. Kaplan, "I haven't seen you since . . . I'm sorry about your wife's passing. Faye was like a second mother to me."

"Yeah," Mr. Kaplan says, gazing wistfully up at his home in the early morning damp summer fog. "She was a wonderful mother." This is what makes him divulge the information about how his son mourns said mom.

So Ray leaves flowers at Faye's grave in front of the Kaplan family obelisk, this time with a signed note that says, *I guess it isn't true that a lady never leaves too soon.* Faye liked to crack jokes starting with, "A lady never," and then end them with something like, "forgets to brush her teeth for *more* than a week," or "presents herself with only one food stain on her pajamas; it's two at a minimum"—whatever it was that made her feel wretched that day. It always made Ray and Noah laugh, so Ray guesses that this reference will at least make Noah smile now that she's gone.

The third contact is a return volley from Noah, a birthday card for Ray on the 11th. It's signed formally (his full name and middle initial and everything), and it says, *You are not acting your age.* Ray is seventeen.

Touché, Ray thinks. That's more cryptic than any message Ray would leave. Is it meant to discourage him, or congratulate him, or to just acknowledge his actions? Indecipherable. Ray moves on to his last shot.

The third and final step is an in-person meeting. He's reminded Noah that no one knows him as well as Ray does and still likes him so much, and he's also highlighted their shared history (Noah will never make another friend his mother approves of, he *can't*), and now it's time to just be friends again. For real this time, not like last time. Last time, Ray thought he could do a little better than Noah, and either Ray overestimated himself (no) or he underestimated

Noah. That's a compliment if he can just phrase it right, Ray knows it.

He executes an opposite approach on Noah than the one that worked on Mr. Kaplan. Noah is back at the University of Chicago, back in his old habits so deeply that he made himself the same schedule Ray once memorized to pursue him the first time, and Ray waits to catch Noah coming home from school. He sits on the splintery bus bench that Noah will disembark at, and lets Noah spot him. Noah freezes when he sees Ray sitting ankle-over-knee at the bench, and he's jostled by the people trying to get off the bus behind him. They push Noah forward enough that the boy walks up and sits beside Ray. They wait for the other commuters to disperse before saying anything.

"I miss her," Noah says, at the same moment Ray is volunteering, "I've missed you."

They're both hit a second late by the other one's statement, and the awkwardness of it makes them both smile, and look away in embarrassment. A year apart and it already feels like old times to Ray.

"Do you wanna rob my frat house this fall?" Ray wants to do it himself, but he also wants to let Noah know that those people and that house mean nothing to him, comparatively.

Noah snorts. "Actually, I kind of do. I've always disliked that place."

"It'll be my last chance to do something drastic there and then watch the aftermath. Even though my grades sucked this year, I've still got enough credits to graduate at eighteen. The youngest grad in the school's history."

"And your plans after that?"

Ray shrugs. "Chicago again, probably grad school or something. What track is your future on now?"

"I'm in the law school here, taking extra classes this summer, and I'm applying to Harvard and Yale among many others over the next six months or so."

Ray smiles and looks at Noah, and he crosses his arms over a strange sense of pride. Noah will get into one of those schools, he truly will, and he'll be a big ol' lawyer any minute after that. Ray really does like this kid.

"You think you'll include the robbery in any of your application essays?"

Noah rolls his eyes. "Maybe I'll talk about the contract I'd make you sign guaranteeing reciprocity before I'd ever agree to join you," he says, standing up and looking down at Ray, considering him. He cocks his head, inviting Ray to walk with him before he goes on saying, "In fact, that wouldn't be bad practice for me, mocking up a contract, regardless of whether its contents are legal or not."

"I'd sign it either way," Ray promises. "Although what I just said is a verbal contract, right? Does that count?"

"Oral contract, and actually that's an interesting question."

Noah launches into a lecture on the subject as Ray walks him home.

2

WRITING IN SANSKRIT THAT EVENING, with Ray waiting on the bed just two feet to Noah's left for his friend to tie up some homework, Noah makes a personal note to himself: *You take up with Ray Klein like he's a bad habit.* After that he stops writing, closes a few books, and pivots in his desk chair to get a full view of Ray.

Ray's looking up at the ceiling like there's something pleasant to see there, instead of a dusty ceiling fan and a slight superficial crack running away from it. His hair is shorter than when Noah last saw him, it's more shorn on the sides, more military, more masculine. It's not long enough to bend into that wave Noah likes to look at. That's probably not the only thing that's changed about him in the year or so they've been at different schools, having different lives.

"What are you so happy about?" Noah asks him. Noah probably feels happy too; he thinks that's the emotion underneath a very wobbly apprehension. Part of him thinks this is all a trick, a bet Ray made with himself just for the sport of seeing if he could wile someone smart back to his own ruin, back into a cesspool he's already crawled out of once before.

"Being back in your room is more of a homecoming than getting back in mine was; how fucked up is that?"

"You can thank yourself for that, you said you didn't want that place to be your home when you left. It's why you left."

Ray's smile deepens, and he cuts his eyes at Noah, and then he reaches out a hand and sets the palm of it on the inside of Noah's left leg, just above the knee.

Noah stays silent as Ray's thumb starts making small back-and-forth strokes. His face feels like it's suffered a sunburn, when all that's really happened is a ferocious blush. Once Ray notices that, and the hitch in Noah's breath, he lifts up on his elbow and starts to reach further up Noah's leg. That causes Noah to throw himself out of his chair. He stands in the middle of his room, his back to Ray, dizzy for a moment, but miraculously not embarrassed at long last. He collects himself enough to step up and lock his bedroom door.

He turns back around and looks Ray in the eyes, a pair of chameleon eyes, the sort of hazel that takes on the color of things around them. Ray is sitting up, shoving the sheets down, getting ready for Noah, and Noah is pulling his feet from his shoes and stripping off his summer blazer—basically making himself comfortable, something that Ray did the second he walked into Noah's house.

Noah crawls over the footboard as gracelessly as a flamingo once he's untucked his shirt and gotten rid of his belt. Ray opens up his posture a little, presenting the front of his body, but Noah wants to try something different this time.

He shakes his head, and twirls a finger, indicating that he wants Ray to turn over. This Ray does, hanging his face and arm off the side of the bed while Noah lays himself closer, and touches the back of Ray's head. Tragically short or not, his hair is still as soft as Noah remembers.

Noah can see enough to see that Ray's eyes are closed, pretending to sleep. That works for him. He caresses from the side of Ray's head down his neck and back, lifts up his shirt enough to get access to his skin, and then tugs at his jeans—just the outer pants—until Ray breaks the ruse of sleep enough to unbutton and start removing them. Noah finishes for him so Ray can go back to his slack position. It's strange to Noah that he only feels like he can be with Ray when Ray pretends he isn't there—eyes averted and mouth shut. The boy's just too good a liar for Noah to really trust those ports of access to his personality, but this way he can be with Ray without the niggling suspicion that he's being fooled. Why would Ray ever put up with this if he didn't like Noah? This is no lie.

Noah leaves the underwear on both of them, but the skin above and below is exposed enough for real, warm contact, and the pressing and thrusting he does through the underwear, that doesn't feel as hampered as it looks. The heat and the crevice and the squeeze of it all is enough to make Noah lose more head than one. And when he's done, and the sweat is evaporating, and his breathing re-regulates into a normal rhythm against Ray's neck, that is when Ray 'wakes up' and rolls over to face Noah again.

They both pull their shirts down because the air-conditioned room is starting to feel chilly, but they pull the covers over their legs and kick their pants fully off underneath.

"How weird do you feel?" Noah asks him.

"No weirder than I always feel. What about you?"

Noah just shakes his head. Not weird at all. He's never felt this at peace with his own body, it's like the perfection of Ray's body can literally rub off on his. Or something like that, since Noah's the one who . . . whatever. Noah laughs a little. For once he doesn't care about the exact way to phrase it. That's a new measure of peace as well.

Ray smiles to see his friend catch a fit of the giggles.

"You haven't been laughing much since she died, have you?"

Noah's smile shrinks a little, but stays on his face. "No, I haven't. You remembered that tulips were her favorite flowers, that's why you got them for her grave, isn't it? And the note you left, that was really—" Ray pops a kiss onto Noah's lips (they've never kissed on the lips before), probably because Noah's voice is starting to tremble. He can't talk about his mother without that crying tremor trying to burble out of him, that's why he hasn't said more than a word about her to anyone but Ray. Since Faye's death, his father and brothers have grown into talking about her fondly, but Noah still can't. He just listens to what they have to say, and that's enough for him, usually.

The kiss from Ray is one long, one short, which Noah realizes is an N in Morse Code. He responds to Ray's message with one of his own: short, long, short; an R. Then he's smirking at his own secret joke—at last he's the one thinking of something mysterious that Ray doesn't understand! How rewarding.

"Now, what are *you* so happy about," Ray states, repeating Noah's question from before, but not really asking it himself because he sits up and pulls his pants back on and moves to the desk chair while Noah redresses himself.

They both seem to agree that what Ray doesn't know can't hurt him.

3

THE BOYS ARE BACK ON SUPERIOR terms, but Ray still has a lot of free time over this last summer of his legal youth. With Noah taking classes in law and teaching classes in birding, the kid stays ceaselessly busy all through the rest of June. They talk quite a bit, many late nights on the phone when Ray is up late staggering home from a campus party and Noah is staying up all night before an early morning birding expedition because he thinks he's sharper when he's not overly rested.

"No doctor would agree with you on that," Ray tells him, chatting about Noah's day before he wants to launch into a discussion of his own.

"You are mistaken. Studies of the napping habits of men like Edison and Churchill—"

"Are you trying to put me to sleep right now?"

Noah scoffs and Ray enters his house through the back door, the one closest to the stairs that are closest to his room, hoping not to get nagged about his exploits the next morning. The nerve his family has lecturing him on being immature for a college man when they're the ones who engineered him to become a college man so young . . . astounding. Noah doesn't have to put up with crap like that, but then Noah is also fast to remind Ray that he doesn't drink or party like Ray does, so. That's a firm point in a debate that they never declare won.

"So, do you want to hear about the bird I bagged tonight?"

"Do you mean like a girl, and do you mean you managed to touch a base or score a basket or whatever the sports metaphor is for that stuff?"

Ray yelps a laugh that nearly becomes a hiccup and certainly ruins all his care in trying to use the quiet entrance in returning home so late. He promised himself that tonight he would actually bathe before he passed out, but since he can't take the phone into the shower, Ray lets go of that fantasy and settles for just getting his pants off. They'd been half off once before, earlier in the night, that was the news he had for Noah.

"She actually believed me when I told her I sold drugs, just mother's prescription meds and ADHD pills to other students, but still. She seemed to think I was some kind of master criminal, and I guess she had a thing for that. She actually tried to blow me."

"What do you mean, 'tried'? What stopped such a thing from being successfully accomplished?"

"Man, if you have to ask, you might never know." Truly, and this truth is already in a locked place in his mind where Ray sticks his most uncomfortable nightmares and disheartening failures, he couldn't seem to enjoy himself. He started off so excited when she leaned in and went for his zipper with this knowing look in her eye, like she had some skill, some secret, something real behind the crumby black mascara that didn't work on her blonde eyelashes. But Ray's excitement hadn't been the right kind, and it didn't translate to a rush of blood to the right place, and the whole experience felt gluey and embarrassing, and the way she let it fall out of her mouth after a minute like a tasteless wad of gum . . . well, Ray won't tell that story to anyone, not even himself. He's already modifying it so that if he ever remembers this night far in the future, he won't really remember which details are true and which are fabricated. And since there is nothing good or bad but thinking makes it so, someday the truth will be what Ray wants it to be.

"Do you think a man or a woman would be inherently better at doing that? Obviously practice goes into the ability at a certain point, and probably women get more practice in general, but there's also the consideration that it takes one to know one, like a man would know better what a man wants."

"Maybe you should go out and collect some data on that," Ray says.

"Hmm. A scientist shouldn't be his own test subject. Maybe you'll find out and lend me some anecdotal evidence."

"Maybe," Ray says. He can admit to being that curious about himself, and what could letting a man give it a try do, be worse? More humiliating? At least when another fellow says, Don't worry, it happens to all guys sometimes, it would be easier for Ray to believe the lie. How can a girl say that with any authority? Maybe she's the common denominator that skews the stats!

"What are your plans this weekend?" Ray is debating even getting up to turn off his light before he conks out, but since he never bothers redecorating when he comes 'home' from school, the walls are hopelessly sad and bare and bright.

"Birding class with that Girl Scout troop, and my aunt's coming over for dinner with her new beau, she's ready to introduce him to the family. What about you?"

"Nothing, I guess. Want to set another fire on the fourth of July?"

"You know the answer to that. Besides, I'm going to some company guy's barbecue with my dad."

"And the week after that you're headed back to Michigan for that bird thing, and that's going to be like a week of camping, right?"

"At least, but Professor Woodrow thinks we're close to finding the bird's nesting ground. Last season we saw where they'd been, and—"

"We'll have to meet up after that some time."

"Yeah. Definitely," Noah says so firmly that Ray knows he means it.

4

"You would have hated this trip," Noah tells Ray on the other side of a supremely successful expedition to find the nesting grounds of Kirtland's warbler. "I loved it, I got so close to the nest I was feeding the parents. The male bird actually hopped on me a few times he was so comfortable. The other guys didn't have the nerve to approach, they were afraid of getting pecked at."

"Were you pecked at?" Ray asks, and Noah raises his sleeve like he has a badge of honor to show off. There are little dotted scars from the female's beak—she was not as comfortable with a human interloper as her colorful counterpart was. The male specimen seemed to like the convenience of having Noah hunt bugs and grubs for his nest, rather than having to do all the work himself. Noah was training the bird into a bad dependent habit, but they only spent three days observing and filming the nest, then they took only pictures and left only footprints.

"It's only the third confirmed finding of a nesting ground in the records, and it's the most recent one for years, scholars thought the birds were dying out because they weren't breeding anywhere. Dr. Woodrow is going to help me get a

L . A . F I E L D S

paper published in a journal somewhere, it's actually a real discovery."

Ray is listening to all this across the table from Noah at a diner staffed with improv actors whose job it is to insult you inoffensively as they seat and serve you. He and Ray were supposed to meet a third party here, but their friend bailed at the last minute, and so now they're on what their waitress characterizes as, "Wow, one of you must be a cheap date." Noah hoped that Ray's policy of never being seen alone in public together wouldn't follow them home, that what happened in Michigan would stay in Michigan, but Ray insists on keeping it going in Chicago too.

And yet, here they are! Their friend Ricky, someone they both knew the year before the transfer to Michigan by virtue of having the same law-ish pre-requisites to take, cancelled on them for some reason attached to his new girlfriend. That is awkward enough, especially after the way their waitress teased them, but now Noah's been jabbering incessantly about a birding trip that Ray has never shown interest in. He admits that to Ray, in an attempt to segue into a more mutual conversation.

"I've been talking a blue streak, haven't I?" Noah asks. Ray probably wishes they had more food on the table, since Noah won't talk and chew at the same time (he was raised with manners).

"What's the origin of the phrase 'blue streak,' is it a speed trail thing?" Ray asks. He's attempting a better conversation too, if he's asking Noah about his other obsessive hobby.

"I feel like it's got to do with lightning? I don't know," Noah says.

Ray pulls out his phone to look it up, and that's when the waitress reapproaches, leans her elbows on the table in an overly ingratiating manner, and says to Noah, "I'd ask if you two wanted a dessert, but with the way he's ignoring you, it must not be going so well. You want an Ed Debevic's paper hat to color like we give to the kids?"

That makes Ray yelp a laugh without looking up from his phone. "How about one banana split with two spoons so I can make it up to him?"

"You got it, Toots," she says, shooting two fake finger guns at them both like she's doing a Yosemite Sam impression.

Noah thinks about asking, *What happened to the no couple's behavior policy?* But he doesn't have the training to tease without affronting like the waitress does, and he doesn't want to question something that pleases him so much anyway.

"I can't find any answer for sure," Ray says, finally dropping the phone from his face. "It's an Americanism though."

"That makes sense, we're a very clever and inventive people when it comes to language."

"So what about executing that frat project the night of the homecoming game? The guys get extra sloppy on nights like that. Stuff's unlocked, strangers are coming and going, and everyone's too drunk to keep track of their valuables."

"Whatever you want," Noah says, hoping Ray gets bored of the idea or can't schedule it right. Noah doesn't want to rob that frat house, there's nothing worth having in there except for Ray, whom he's already regained. Ray assumed that Noah was in for really doing it when he answered him flippantly about the idea at the bus stop, and if Noah tries to take that assurance away from Ray, he'll spoil the good bond they have going again.

"I want way more than that," Ray says as their banana split arrives with two spoons spooning bowls in the middle.

"Enjoy or don't, I don't give a flip," the waitress says as she sets it down.

"You eat it, I don't like fruit on my ice cream," Ray says, getting up. "I'm gonna hit the bathroom."

Noah watches him very closely as he goes, free to stare as long as Ray's back is to him, because otherwise Ray's taken to scolding Noah a bit about how long he looks, and how intensely. Ray still thinks Noah's the only reason there are rumors about them, like it doesn't take two to tango.

It would be a lot more annoying for Noah to be condescended to like that if he didn't catch himself snapping in and out of trances while watching Ray. Noah can't really argue with what's true, regardless of whether or not he likes it.

Noah waves down the waitress.

"Hey, we have to go, and we didn't touch this," Noah says about their dessert. "Obviously we'll still pay for it, but maybe you've got another table that'll want it."

"Maybe," she says. "One check or two?"

So she really can't tell if they're together or not, that's funny; neither can Noah half the time.

5

THE PLAN IS THIS: RAY has engineered it so his frat brothers aren't expecting him until after homecoming weekend. Ray's taking only classes that meet one day a week, and he's already starting this school year off with the right foot forward by skipping the first day (nothing vital is ever covered on the first day). That means he'll have to sneak onto his own campus, and into his own house, late at night after the game and the libations have put everyone's lights out. This will present Ray as the only one with a totally unassailable alibi, which means he will get to be the detective when he officially returns the following Monday and the boys all tell him the wild news: we've been robbed.

"Are you excited?" Ray asks Noah as he hops into the passenger seat just around sunset. It's at least a four hour drive, they'll do it in shifts, take their time, arrive on campus in Noah's car (one that won't be recognized as associated with Ray to ensure that he remains above suspicion), and stake out the frat houses, maybe find another candidate for robbery as they lurk and wait. Noah got rejected by at least one frat house, surely he wouldn't mind injuring them back.

"Stoked," Noah says grumpily. Ray has given him every incentive in the world to actually go through with this. (1) Noah can keep literally anything they take, money especially, no matter the amount. (2) Should anything go wrong they've already thought of an escape hatch—Noah will say he is in Michigan to stop Ray from a fake theft prank, and Ray will admit to that, he's promised. (3) That whole cocksucker rumor got started because of Ray's transition into Greek life, and Ray has told Noah (as even more payment for accompanying him) that they can actually give it a try if he wants to. And he does seem to want to, so that's another upcoming adventure. Maybe he'll have more skill at it than what's-her-face did, and Ray will actually enjoy himself. Weirder things have happened.

The setting sun, though it's no brilliant tropical Technicolor sheet, looks pretty impressive to Ray. The sky is only pink for a minute before that autumnal gray sky snuffs it out, but Ray's akindle with anticipation, he feels like he's crackling with electricity.

"Can you stop bouncing around over there?" Noah asks him at the state line between Illinois and Indiana. "Your foot's been jumping constantly for like an hour, it's driving me fucking crackers."

Ray laughs, steps on one foot with the other, and then starts drumming his fingers. The energy has to go somewhere so it doesn't burst him open. Noah rolls his big eyes and presses his left temple like he's trying to quash a headache.

"Pull over and let me drive for a while," Ray says. "That'll keep me busy."

"No, you'll just speed and then I'll get a ticket."

"You don't have to be so nervous. We planned for every contingency, you said so yourself, you said that this is a perfect crime."

"Everyone in prison right now probably said the same thing at some point."

"Oh, calm down, this isn't even a prison sort of crime. It's a prank, remember? If we get caught, we were just kidding."

"Yeah, you know, just because we're doing it, that doesn't mean we have to talk about it."

And so Ray stops talking about it. Sourpuss over there is starting to ruin the magic that Ray can't come by as easily as he used to. This trip took weeks of cajoling, months of planning, and can't ever happen again—it's a one shot only opportunity, and he can't let Noah taint it.

When they cross into Michigan, Noah is still driving, he wouldn't let go of control long enough for Ray to take a turn. No matter to Ray; he can just take the wheel for the return trip, as if it matters. They park on a dark visitor's lot full of cars and plastic party cups and the detritus of sporting hoopla: cigarette butts and cheap streamers and torn support signs and dropped food.

Ray leaps out like he's come home to a kingdom and a parade, he's so happy they've finally arrived. He drags Noah on at least an hour of fast-paced walking and prowling through the fraternity streets. It's another hour before any of the houses even start to go quiet, and 2 AM before Noah will let Ray head for the door.

Ray wants to break in through a window, but the front door's ajar, it would just be stupid not to use it. Everyone sleeps on the second floor, so Noah and Ray trawl through the ground level: three wallets, one Hermes wristwatch, Ray grabs a beer, and Noah takes a laptop. That's going to hurt whoever left it downstairs, but maybe not so badly. Depending on who the owner is, he might be grateful for the excuse to get an extension on his homework. Ray will be sure to tell whomever it is to look on the bright side when he returns on Monday.

They stash their loot in Noah's car and take one more stroll through the Greek row part of the neighborhood.

"Okay, that wasn't so bad," Noah says.

"What about that house that dissed you, let's check to see if they leave their doors open!"

"We don't know the layout of that house," Noah says, but Ray remembers which one it was, and he remembers that he once thought it was too close to him when Noah mentioned it back during their rough patch.

"Come on, look," Ray says, his voice a thrilled whisper even though they're on an empty street with no one in hearing distance at all. "That's an open window, just go snag something out of it, you'll be happy you did once you're back in Chicago, please? Don't you think it's always better to regret something done than something left undone—"

"Oh, for fuck's sake," Noah grumbles as he veers suddenly into the yard of the house, reaches to pluck something out of the window, and returns immediately to Ray's side. "If you're going to get so philosophical, here, happy?"

He hands Ray a TV's remote control, and Ray almost reaches full hysteria just looking at it, just imagining those guys never being able to find the remote again, blaming each other, never even once considering they were robbed of such a small, insignificant item.

"You always make me happy," he says through laughing gasps, wiping at his leaking eyes.

And through the blear Ray sees that this comment finally gets Noah to smile. It's the first time he's smiled all night.

6

NOAH WISHES HE COULD TAKE a picture of this whole ride home from Michigan, from this most recent felony. If all of Ray's simpering, shallow friends could see the boy like this, they'd understand why he has only one close friend, and why that friend is so strange. Even Noah's brothers might understand, for though they want the best for their youngest baby bro, they still think that Ray's somehow too good for him. Nobody ever sees Ray under the full crush of a desire achieved, and thus gone forever.

Ray is still in the passenger seat, slumped so far down he'd be on the floor if a seatbelt wasn't holding him up. Noah wouldn't let him drive during the approach because his jittery form of quickness—so charming in small doses, like the way he bounds into rooms or drums with his silverware—was on the dangerous end of the scale: shaky hands that couldn't hold a cigarette even if Noah would let him smoke one in the car, and a tapping foot so fast and violent it made parts of the car vibrate out of tune with the engine. That excitement Ray has is easy for him to contain within normal societal parameters most of the time, but the downswing of that height is this: he looks like a puppet with no tension in his strings.

Noah reaches for the radio, but Ray heaves up enough energy to swat Noah away from the dashboard. Noah feels his lips purse, tries not to hold it against the boy because these sorts of slumps happen to all the greatest men, real and fictional. Noah tries to amuse Ray with an anecdote about one character he particularly likes.

"You know, maybe you are more like Sherlock Holmes than I am, he was the same way after he solved a case, manic to the point of self-destruction, and then bottomlessly empty, incommunicado."

Ray looks over at him, and becomes communicado enough to pull out the cigarettes he was begging Noah to smoke on the first side of the trip, and lights one even though he knows he's not allowed.

Noah sighs, and sneezes hazardously at the wheel of a long drive, which just makes him more frustrated with Ray's weakness. For being the most remarkable person Noah has ever met, he's still far from perfect.

"If you're going to be an asshole after I've done everything you wanted all night, at least open a window." Noah uses the driver's side controls to put down the passenger and back seat windows, then flips the switch that locks out the passenger side's controls so Ray can't change the configuration.

"Don't pretend you did it out of the goodness of your heart, you expect payment."

"You agreed to an exchange, the same as I did. We're both over eighteen now, we're finally adults all over the world, I expect both of us to be able to act as such."

"The way you talk is unbelievably pompous. Are you so afraid people won't believe you're studying law that you have to talk like you're in front of a judge?"

Ray tries to blow smoke into Noah's face, even though the wind through the car is strong enough to carry it away. It's just a sign of disrespect. Eighteen or not, he looks more like a child than ever; a resentful sneer on his face and moonlight bleaching his hair to the point that he has a crown like a Long-Tailed Tyrant. He's dipping his head in and out of the open window, probably enjoying the feel of the breeze on a great night for him, all while Noah chauffeurs him around with a cough now, another reaction to the smoke.

"No wonder your mother can't stand you," Noah tells him, sad more than angry at this point. "You get everything you want and still act like a brat."

"So why did your mother like me so much? What was she, stupid?"

"She liked you because I like you. And she didn't know you like I do, she never met you like this."

Ray snorts out the last puff of his cigarette like a raging bull and returns to a properly seated position. After about a mile of silence, hopefully some reflective time where Ray is appreciating that even during a fight Noah manages to like him at his worst, Ray snaps slightly out of it.

"Unlock the passenger controls, let me roll up the windows, it's fucking cold."

Noah does this, and Ray seals the car back up. Then he turns on the heat and the radio in apology.

"I just don't know what I can do after this," Ray confesses. "Arson and robbery and burglary: done. So now what? Kidnapping, rape, murder? Where do I go from here?" This is what's bothering him, Noah knows. He's got the same problem on his side of the deal—after what Noah wants to try on Ray for this crime, another step further would be pretty extreme. It's a problem they warn every new law student about, in fact: never ask a question you don't already know the answer to. It's a rule that serves one well in a courtroom, but out here in the wilds of life? It's not even what Ray says to avoid telling Noah how lackluster his other sexual exploits are: *If you have to ask, you'll never know.* Noah should have called bullshit on that tired line, because that's never been true between the two of them. You *have* to ask, and risk embarrassment and refusal, otherwise you'll never know how disappointing even getting what you want can be.

And yet even on this unsatisfactory ride home, Noah would rather regret the things he's done than regret never even trying, Ray was right with that cliché tonight. Ray believes in that too, he has that same sort of courage, and that's why they still put up with each other.

7

THE FOLLOWING MONDAY, RAY RETURNS to Michigan. He drives the four hours alone, with his own car full of clothes and technology, chain-smoking with the reckless abandon of being able to set his own limits, which is why he overdoes it, and arrives back at the ZBT house feeling sort of faint and sick. On a normal day, at least two people would have told him he's looking green around the gills, especially since he actually did fall into a faint on initiation day, mostly due to nerves, and because the others shocked him by bagging his head and tackling him to the floor. Naturally no one wants to let Ray forget that, but the house is still in a tizzy after being robbed. That fact (and a cold soda) perk Ray up again.

It was Lebowitz who left his computer downstairs, who is sitting at the coffee table now cussing at his old leftover laptop, trying to load his last backup from a hard drive onto an antique. There is an air of dampened spirit in the room, just about everyone lost something, even if it was only a wallet that was empty of money but still full of plastic that must be replaced. The kid who lost his watch is the saddest—he's a new member, and it was his high school graduation present, and his parents are giving him a royally hard time about it. His upperclassman mentor isn't helping him feel better at all, mostly because Schwartz over there has been robbed too, and he has two other little fledglings ('pledglings' is how Ray and Noah think of them), and he has so many to ignore because they didn't trust Ray as a mentor. His age was the least of it; between his erratic grades, and more than one official sanction against him for the drinking, and the probable assumption that he cheats at cards (no one can be *that* lucky), they didn't trust him with a young, impressionable mind. So be it then: serves everybody right to suffer for not being better friends to Ray.

"What the hell happened to you guys?" Ray asks. He's smiling wide because he knows the answer. They think he's smiling because he doesn't.

"Looks like you had fun," Schwartz says. "We were robbed."

"No way," Ray says with a drawl. Does his ecstasy sound like a normal person's disbelief?

"Yes way," Lebowitz says spitefully. "I'm already so sick of talking about it."

"Then someone else tell me," Ray says, looking at the new kid—what's his name, Todd or Tim or some shit?—hoping that he'll get to hear the saddest story in the room. To think, half of that money's in his own pocket, and that watch is on Noah's wrist . . . Ray has all the thrill of being a spy in enemy territory.

The guys try to ruin his fun, they see no beauty in tragedy, and they don't want to tell their stories more than once, nobody but Lebowitz and Tim Tam over there even reported their losses to the campus police. They don't want to even speculate on the mystery of who the thief could be, everyone agrees it was 'some asshole' and that's as far a depth as they want to plumb.

"Did you ever consider it might have been a girl? Some siren bitch one of you thought you had a chance with, huh?"

No one is in the mood to be teased, and after that comment, people start to leave the common area or scowl at Ray, so he calls out a platitudinous "sorry for everyone's loss," and unpacks his car. After making sure the car is totally empty and moving it from the unloading spot, Ray pulls out his phone and takes a walk.

This is what he needs Noah for, why he insists on dragging him along on crimes, and why he remembers to humor the guy's proclivities. Ray's putting off that thing Noah wants to do until his next trip home—they were too sick of each other after the drive back to Chicago, even Noah wanted some time apart—but with the thrill of what he's done returned to Ray's heart today, he has to explode his good vibes towards somebody, otherwise they'll shake him apart.

"What?" is how Noah answers the phone, but at least he answers it.

"Did I apologize yet for my demeanor Saturday night? Because I'm over it."

"Back in Michigan?" Noah asks. "Happy again?"

"Noah, really, they're such idiots, and you know none of them wants to take any responsibility for leaving doors unlocked and valuables unattended. Like, who would you and me be the angriest with if we got robbed?"

"Ourselves, of course. That quality of self-awareness and personal responsibility is a part of what makes us so superior to everyone else."

"And it gives us the right to take their shit, isn't that your Nietzschean thinking?"

"What right? If they deserved to keep their possessions, they would have guarded them better. If you want to think of it charitably, you might say we've taught them a valuable life lesson. They'll be locking doors for the rest of college at least, don't you think?"

Listening to Noah reason like this is music to Ray's ears, he's got his head tipped to the phone at his ear like there's a lullaby coming through it. He can take Ray's thoughts and translate them into poetry sometimes.

"Yeah, I do think," he agrees amiably. "So, Michigan's fall break is in October, so I'll be back in Chicago then for sure, if not earlier."

"I've looked it up, your school's break is the second week of October, mine is the third. We have an overlapping weekend."

"I'll see you then," Ray says instead of goodbye. A deal's a deal.

8

NOAH DIDN'T KNOW WHICH WEEKEND he desired Ray's return from Michigan to occur on. Was the sooner the better? Or Halloween weekend, since they have such fond memories of that holiday together? Or Noah's birthday, in late November? Could he stand to wait so long for his reward? Or would the dread of what he wanted to try make putting it off for a while all the easier to stomach?

Ray was the only one who could decide when he would come home, Noah knows he worried about it for nothing. He scolded himself whenever his mind wandered off his books and started to woolgather so pathetically, but still he did it.

When the date is finally set in mid-October, Noah can't help but give over to the Humanities in himself. As the day approaches, he sets himself to reading and even memorizing poetry, and he's jotting some down while he awaits Ray's autumnal arrival, writing the lines in their own native English, just because he feels that it was said right the first time. He has been ruminating particularly on a snippet of a James Baldwin poem called "Munich, Winter 1973," which is more on-the-nose regarding Noah's current situation than he's even comfortable exploring:

> The streets, I observe,
> are wintry.
> It feels like snow.
> Starlings circle in the sky,
> conspiring,
> together, and alone,
> unspeakable journeys
> into and out of the light.
>
> I know
> I will see you tonight.
> And snow
> may fall
> enough to freeze our tongues
> and scald our eyes.
> We may never be found again!
>
> Just as the birds above our heads
> circling
> are singing,
> knowing
> that, in what lies before them,
> the always unknown passage,
> wind, water, air,
> the failing light
> the falling night
> the blinding sun

they must get the journey done.
Listen.
They have wings and voices
are making choices
are using what they have.
They are aware
that, on long journeys,
each bears the other,
whirring,
stirring
love occurring
in the middle of the terrifying air.

Ray comes over on this chilly evening wearing a spring coat instead of a fall one because he didn't pack right for the weekend back home. Noah sees him from the living room window where he's been monitoring the street for half an hour, just waiting on Ray to skip on over from his house. Ray sees Noah through the window, sloppily salutes him through the glass, then walks to the front door and lets himself in. He joins Noah in the living room, sits on the windowsill as near to Noah as he can get without sitting in his lap. He gets straight to logistics.

"Who's home?"

"Nobody before eight o'clock." His father is working, and his brothers are working—everyone has jobs except the baby of the family.

"Your room, I assume?" Ray's arms are crossed, his back against what must be a very cold window pane. He hasn't looked directly at Noah since walking inside, but Noah's been scrutinizing him.

"It has to be."

"Should we do this first and see if we can stand each other after?"

"Who says I can stand you now?" Noah asks, standing up and leading the way.

It's awkward before it even commences, this act of which they already stand accused and convicted. If only the procedural defense of double jeopardy could exempt them from having to experience this for the first time, but alas: autrefois convict, though they are not yet guilty.

With the door locked and Ray unzipped and tossed upon the bed with his arm across his eyes, Noah gives it a try. His problems: too many teeth, too many taste buds, and the unceasing necessity to breathe. Ray's problems: he's a windsock and not a weathervane, and there's a grumbling noise in his throat that can't be anything if it's not partially disgust, and he's not limp anywhere except the one spot where he shouldn't be. His body is tense, his lips pressed tightly together, and the cords in his neck are standing in what (given the circumstances) should not be called relief.

Noah can't be sure who quits first, whether it's his gag reflex or Ray's that makes them separate, that makes Ray pull back while Noah sticks out his tongue in the same way he used to push chewed vegetables out of his mouth as a child. Ray sits against Noah's bedroom wall, he buttons up, and he knuckles his forehead with a mirrored swiping motion to the one Noah uses to wipe his mouth.

Noah sits beside Ray, knows better than to try and touch him at all, and scoffs out a small laugh. He's just as displeased as Ray was when he got what *he* wanted the night of the burglary! They make quite a pair of Agapornis, don't they?

"That was no better than when that girl tried it, was it?"

"No," Ray says. "You didn't seem happy about it either."

"No, I wasn't."

Ray grimaces and shrugs. "Never again, right?"

"Not that, no thank you."

The politeness of Noah's response catches Ray by surprise, and once it gets him laughing, Noah starts to smile too.

"Maybe what we have is more of a folie à deux sort of thing, purer than all this sort of basal activity."

"That's French, what you just said? It doesn't mean love, does it?"

Noah shakes his head and finally gets enough eye contact from Ray to give him a sardonic look. "Madness," he informs his friend.

"That I agree with!" Ray says, jumping from the bed and striding toward the door. Sex or not, whatever this was, he still wants a cigarette after it.

They are standing out on the lanai next, Noah keeping Ray company while he smokes, and keeping him standing when the smoke and possibly the excitement of the evening cause him to slump against the back door.

"Feeling weak?" Noah teases.

"All I had for breakfast was scotch. I can't recommend trying that"—he gestures towards the second floor of the house—"on an empty stomach. It's like trying to donate blood without having breakfast first."

"If you say so. I think for some people, what I was doing would work just fine on an empty stomach."

"You're revolting," Ray says, amused though he is at the dirty talk, and still using Noah's shoulder to brace himself.

"That makes me a revolutionary," Noah says, happy to watch Ray's swirling mind try to figure out what he's talking about. "Think about it," he says, flapping Ray's spring coat at the lapels in the hopes that the chill air will continue to restore him. "Don't revolutionaries revolt?"

When Ray rolls his eyes without toppling over, Noah knows that he, and they, are fine.

9

For some reason, Ray's best friend gets a birthday party no nineteen-year-old boy would ever want. Noah's father and his three brothers and literally the whole neighborhood gather at the Kaplan family home for this shindig. It's less about Noah getting older and more about this being the first celebrated festive occasion since his mother died. Ray's parents are invited before he himself is, technically, and they actually walk over to the Kaplan's with their son, dressed nice and holding wine and flowers and a covered dish made by their cook.

Mother and Father don't speak on the entire stroll. Mother is holding the wine and flowers because she is worried about the food spilling onto or steaming her blouse, at least that was what she lectured to her husband about before leaving the house.

The Kleins arrive with the same fake smile spreading across three faces. Their neighbors from their north side (the ones who occasionally snitch on

Ray for coming and going at all hours) are standing in the same corner with their southern-side neighbors, a couple of Jewish Christians who look as uncomfortable as they must feel everywhere. Mrs. Rosen and her extremely rare husband are talking to Noah Senior, probably paying their respects. The grandson they're babysitting for the weekend is the only life at the party, he's jumping around the room soaking up a lot of attention. Ray's mother asks the boy how he likes school, trying to be polite. Robbie says he doesn't like school.

"Nobody likes school," Ray murmurs at her before going to find the birthday boy, the only person he knows who actually does seem to like school, or at least learning.

Ray spots Noah shaking hands with people in the study. It takes five minutes for Noah to extricate himself, and Ray watches him for the duration; Noah's all puffed up and stiff and proper, like an inflated bullfrog. When he finally comes over to shake Ray's hand (weird), Ray asks him, "Is there any bird that looks like a frog? Because you'd be that one."

"Birds eat frogs, they don't resemble them," Noah says before he's pulled away again.

The so-called party clears out within an hour. Noah's father prepares a weak hot toddy for each of his sons, plus one for Ray, who stays after his parents go home. They all toast to Noah's last year as a teenager.

"Finally," Noah says before he takes a tiny sip of what Ray swallows whole without thinking of how it must look. "I've been a teenager for *years*, I'm sick of it by now."

Noah's father laughs, and his two older brothers smile and check the time before getting back to their own lives.

Mr. Kaplan sighs contentedly. He glances at Ray before saying to Noah, "I know your mother's proud of who you've become."

"I know that too," Noah says with a small flinch in the corner of his mouth. His father hugs him and departs.

Noah sets his forehead on Ray's shoulder. Ray walks out from under that familiarity to pour himself a real helping of whiskey.

"It's my birthday," Noah says, like that will convince Ray to walk back over and continue to get touched.

"It is. That's why I have something for you." The whiskey warms its way into Ray's muscles, and he sits down in front of the study's fireplace, where a small flame is dying out.

"A present?"

"A proposition. I think we should kill someone."

"Really?" Noah says pleasantly. He doesn't realize how serious Ray is about this. Ray leaps to close the door, then returns to the fireside where Noah has sat down and is helping himself to a sip of Ray's drink.

"I've been thinking about it; murder is the ultimate crime, isn't it? If I can commit a perfect murder, I don't have to do any of this small time shit anymore. No more insecurity, no more playing pattycakes, a real crime makes me a real criminal forever."

"That's sort of a strange ambition, don't you think? Why don't you get a graduate degree instead? You know if you're the right kind of lawyer you can murder people publically, on behalf of the state."

"That wouldn't be the same."

"Become the executioner then."

"And spend all that time working in a prison just hoping they'll pick me to flip the switch someday? I might as well kill someone the old fashioned way if I'm willing to go through all that, I don't see much of a difference there."

"Everyone else does. Don't you want the respect of your peers?"

"What peers? I thought you and me were Übermensch?"

"Übermenschen," Noah corrects, but he raises his eyebrows and nods once, his way of ceding the point. He makes a summoning gesture to Ray's drink, and Ray gives it to him; let him have the whole thing! There's no drug yet invented that can make Ray feel as good as this idea does.

"And you want me involved in this?" Noah asks.

"Yes," Ray says, leaning closer, his forearms on his knees. "I need you involved with this. It's kind of a serious task, I want my best people on it."

Noah lets out a hum, a sound very near a laugh.

"And before you say no, just keep in mind our system of trade. This is the only crime I want to perpetrate from now on, so it's this or nothing."

Noah sighs. "Understood. Although if I agree to this, I bet you'll be sorry you made such a deal when the time comes for me to collect."

Ray grins, sure that it's just a matter of time until he has everything he wants.

"I'll live," he says.

10

Noah spends about a week thinking about this, and he writes at least a thousand and one lists about the pros and cons of even humoring Ray's plan, regardless of whether or not Noah would actually participate in it. Encouraging him could be dangerous in itself, you can't promise Ray something and not deliver; his parents did that to him once by not letting him go to Europe, and he'll spend the rest of his life making them sorry for it. Another con about that, if Noah lies to him deliberately, he and Ray won't be friends ever again. And killer or not, Ray's still the best friend he's ever had, and Noah won't throw that away lightly.

But it isn't just Ray to consider. Noah and his brothers get an all-family dinner at the bar mitzvah restaurant, a completely unprecedented occasion, all because Noah got into graduate school. Harvard. Harvard Law. Not a joke.

"Our little genius," Mike the oldest calls him. "The baby is always the favorite; I don't see what you could do to screw that up now."

"I bet I could find a way to ruin it," Noah says, his head having been full of the perfect way to destroy a life for weeks. "Or don't you give me any credit for creativity?"

The table laughs, his father hardest of all, because they truly believe Noah's kidding.

The dinner isn't Noah's real reward for this accomplishment either, it's just a fancy way to announce a Kaplan family trip . . . to Europe.

"All my children are adults now, and you make me proud," his father says. "And your mother would've loved the thought of us all abroad for the first time, together."

Invoking Faye is the way to solidify that plan: this summer everyone agrees to take three weeks off to travel together. Paris and Rome, maybe not in that order, they'll decide later. Either way, Ray's going to hate it.

So Noah gets into *the* law school, and he gets the trip to Europe that Ray was robbed of the last time he graduated, and he's going to demur about one measly murder? The one thing Ray really wants, for which he'd happily give up everything that Noah has, if only he could achieve it? Could Noah really say no with any sound logical reasoning? Could he do that to his only friend?

By Thanksgiving, Noah knows what he's going to say. He tells himself, *If anyone could get away with it, it's the teenager who got into Harvard Law School, and if you believe that then you should prove it.* He tells himself, *There's a very good chance Ray will plan and scheme and yet never get around to an actual murder, and all you have to do is put it off until Europe, because there won't be any time for it after that, ever.* He tells Ray during a very brief phone call, "Meet me at Rosehill Cemetery tomorrow at noon, you know which spot."

Ray is already lounging against the Kaplan family obelisk when Noah arrives exactly on time. Ray rises to stand over Faye's grave with him. Noah is staring down at the stone. Ray is not.

"You know, if you want people to visit your final resting place, you should really install a bench. I think I'll mention that to my dad, it's a good idea."

"What killed her used to be called Bright's disease."

"Hmm. There was nothing bright about it."

Noah looks up, looks around, and sighs. "The name Rosehill for this place was an accident. A man named Roe would only sell the land to the city if they named the whole place after him, Roe's Hill, possessive. Some secretary wrote it up wrong, and I bet no one's sorry about that; the dude was being kind of self-important."

"Delusional, too. I don't see any hills around here, do you?"

Noah snorts. Ray can always make him laugh, even when he's in a very fateful mood.

"I'm going to Europe this summer, and Harvard in the fall."

"Jesus!" Ray says with an impressed whistle.

"Why would you call on Jesus in the Jewish section of the cemetery?"

"Because I'm that surprised," Ray says. "And he was Jewish himself, you're the one who told me that, aren't you?"

"I'm pretty sure I taught you everything you know."

"Though certainly not humility," Ray says, nudging Noah out of his stiff posture.

"Certainly not."

"Let's take a walk."

They ramble through the grounds of the bury patch, pausing at interesting grave markers like the leafless stone trees and glass-protected statues to keep the punishing weather away. Eventually they come to a cannon, a war monument with a pyramid of heavy ammunition beside it, and Noah finally says what he came here to say.

"Let's do it," he tells Ray, watching his face carefully as he receives this news. "The ultimate crime, the most dangerous game . . . I'm in, I'll do it with you."

Noah expects sunshine to figuratively burst from Ray's face, but he doesn't believe it yet.

"Why? What makes you want to do this when you don't have to? Just can't stand all your success? Trying to sabotage yourself?"

"I'm trying to stay true to myself. If I'm an atheist like I say, then there's no moral reason not to, and seeing my mother's grave reminds me of that conviction. No loving God would exchange her for me in this world, but that's what happened. And if I'm really a subscriber to Nietzsche, there's no logical reason not to. 'One must not avoid one's tests, although they constitute perhaps the most dangerous game one can play,' that's a direct quote." It's a line followed by cautions about what not to cling to in an effort to avoid the tests that reveal one's true character. Cling not to king or country or science or even one's own freedom: *Not to cleave to one's own liberation, to the voluptuous distance and remoteness of the bird, which always flies further aloft in order always to see more under it—the danger of the flier.* So Noah can't let the possibility of getting caught and going to prison stop him either.

"So, it's all an intellectual exercise for you? You can't think of a reason not to, so you might as well?"

"I have a reason in favor of it, too. Another wise man said, 'the realization of oneself is the prime aim of life, and to realize oneself through pleasure is finer than to do so through pain.' This would give me pleasure because it would give you pleasure, and certainly I'm the only one who would go so far to make you happy."

"I see." Now Ray smiles, not the cocky one he usually has, but hopeful and giddy. "I've got one, I've got a Nietzsche quote, and it's really fitting too: 'What is done out of love always takes place beyond good and evil.' Isn't that right?"

"Right. I mean, correct."

"Two rights make one wrong!" Ray shouts in victory, holding up his hand for a high five. When Noah obliges, Ray lets out a whoop so loud, it scares a small dole of mourning doves out of a nearby tree and away into the sky.

LOST
BOYS

1

RAY'S CRIME OF A LIFETIME begins with a daytrip to Lake Michigan, to people watch and brainstorm about ideal victim demographics. Noah resists it every step of the way.

"I don't know who you think we're going to see at the lake in winter, wouldn't this idea work better in spring? In summer?"

"You're leaving this summer, we're doing this now, and I'm sure there will be people out there, but the point isn't to pick one *today*, it's to speculate on all the different kinds of people who live in this city, and which ones are the most convenient to . . . include in our plan."

Ray is being discreet because they're still on the train—green to red (not the best omen in that transfer) up to Sheridan, for a short walk out to the shore. For some reason the wind off the lake isn't half as bad as it seems to be when it cuts through the buildings and tries to shove one into icy road traffic.

They drag themselves out to the beach with a blanket, a thermos of hot cocoa spiked with vodka, and they sit down in tense, balled-up postures, huddled into themselves for warmth.

"See, there are people out here," Ray says.

One old dude is in the actual water, in a full-body wetsuit. There is a couple with a dog, all three of them wearing sweaters and running around to stay warm. There are people out walking on their lunch break, but most of them stay on the pavement and don't come down onto the mealy sand. It's like a big mess of cold grits out on the sand, that's how a frat brother of Ray's from some Southern state described it. Ray keeps that simile to himself though, since it would only put Noah in a shittier mood.

Noah sighs, already tired of an adventure just begun. He starts speculating first, at least.

"That dude in the water is too tough to try and kill, if even the temperature can't do it. You could probably kill that dog if you caught it after a day like this, when its energy's been run out. It still might fight hard though; animals are always ready to be vicious when threatened."

"People are animals like that," Ray observes.

"Not all of them, and not all the time. Psychology plays a large role in that, just think of Stockholm syndrome, or the Milgram experiment, or the Stanford prison experiment."

"I don't want to think about any of that, I want to think about a victim I can overpower if things go wrong."

"The dog then," Noah says, pulling his knit cap down further over his ears—they're furiously red because of the cold.

"At least no one could believe the dog's word over mine."

"I'd believe a dog over you," Noah mumbles, blowing out another sigh from so deep within that it creates a dense cloud of vapor.

"I was thinking it'd have to be a young girl, or a child. Someone so small that even if they fight and kick, I can still force them around."

Noah rolls his eyes towards his forehead a bit, and nods as he pictures it. His eyes are awfully gray and colorless on most days, but this wintery shore is putting a stormy slate tint into them. They almost look as troubled and queasy as this lake does in December.

"You know, if you want to kill a girl, we could rape her too, then we'd both finally lose that pesky virginity."

"I don't believe you really want to do that," Ray says. Noah's sexuality seems difficult enough with a schedule and a contract and a complacent male partner, he wouldn't be able to stomach a fight with a girl. They'd have to drug her before he could even try.

"Well, do you want to do it? You like the idea of having sex with women, this would be your chance to go all the way. It's what they say in baseball, right? Fourth base, a home run?"

Ray laughs. "Hey, you finally got it right!" Now they're both smiling, and maybe Noah will actually join the party he's already RSVP'd to, if Ray phrases it right.

Ray turns to Noah, and would probably take his hands if he weren't clutching their thermos and leeching its heat, that would make him listen more closely.

"Look, that isn't the crime I want to commit, let's not muddy the waters with that mess. You're thinking of this like it's a chore, but don't, okay? Think about the sense of accomplishment you'll have if we plan this right, plan it neatly, and get away with it! Think about what a rare specimen you'd be then, *nobody* does that."

"Well, nobody we've heard of, if they really got away with it. I mean, by definition—"

"Shut up, Noah. You've agreed to this, and because you're not a liar you're going to do it, and if you're going to do it, then why not do it right?"

"That's a fair point," Noah says.

"Thank you," Ray says, turning back to look out over the water. "I think it'll have to be a kid. And probably not a girl, since what you just said is the first thing people will think, and they'll look for her too hard." Ray sighs contentedly. He has a victim to picture going forward; now he just has to build a crime around that unidentified boy.

Noah stays quiet.

"Okay," Ray says, knowing it's time to reward Noah, since Ray has what he wanted from this trip, an idea to start with. "So tell me about pelicans or seagulls or whatever water birds you're thinking about right now."

"Those are salt water birds, this is a fresh water lake; I hope you know that and are just joking."

"Maybe." Ray probably did know that, but he doesn't often bother to think before he speaks, it's too time consuming.

"They're salt water birds, and so are terns and petrels."

"Turns and petrol, okay."

"And so are cormorants."

"That sounds like a rank in the army to me."

"Not in our army, unless you're confusing the word with colonels."

"Commandant?"

"That's closer, but a cormorant is still a bird."

"Any other salt water birds you want to tell me about?"

Now Noah turns to Ray, the closest expression he has to a smirk on his face, which means he looks like he's about to spit out a marble.

"Penguins."

They both start chortling after that, and Ray says, "That's funny because it's so cold."

"It's funnier because we're about to experience a polar vortex in Chicago."

"You should quit murder after this and go into comedy."

"*That's* funny because the aim is actually 'to kill' in both professions."

"You're killing me right now," Ray tells him, standing up and wobbling as the spiked cocoa makes its presence in his body known. "Let's get out of here before we freeze to death."

2

"HAVE YOU THOUGHT ABOUT THE method of apprehension?" Noah asks. He doesn't really want to prompt Ray at this endeavor, but it is fascinating to watch his mind fail to work up to the most obvious problems. They're spending a bright winter's day in the International Museum of Surgical Science because when the weather's nice, museums are empty. Plus, Ray is on a mission to completely desensitize himself to the horrors of the human body. "Because if you want to kill someone without a gun," Noah continues, "you'll probably have to be close to them, and in a private place. Wait, do you know how you want to do it yet?"

"Not a gun," Ray says. "Too loud, too easy, and I doubt those birding pistols you have could kill a person."

"If you shot them right through the eye, aiming at the brain," Noah points to a replica skull of Phineas Gage for illustration, "you could do it, probably. If not kill, then certainly maim."

"Yeah, see, failure is not an option. I read somewhere that people even screw up suicides with guns, though I don't know how."

Noah motioned to the plaque under Phineas as something of an answer itself, and says, "Nobody knows exactly how, the brain is a mysterious thing. But suicides could go wrong a hundred ways, like I know at least one case of a man living through a self-induced shotgun blow to the neck."

"Okay, how the fuck? Don't shotguns spray?" Ray made a gesture, trying to illustrate the expansion of buckshot from a cartridge. It looks like he's auditioning for Chicago the musical: jazz hands!

Noah explains. "Think of how long a shotgun is, how hard it is to reach the trigger. So this guy wanted to blow his head off, and he put the muzzle, which is a cute word for it, right here." He reaches over to Ray's neck, to touch the spot where a medical professional might take a pulse. Ray tries to dodge him a little, but the room, the whole museum, is as dead and empty as every surgical mishap they've seen today, so Noah insists, and touches Ray's neck with his first two fingers, and pokes them in hard. "He pushed the barrel in so far that he shoved his windpipe to one side and his jugular to the other, and when he pulled the trigger, all he did was paralyze himself."

"Damn," Ray says, swatting Noah's hand away now that the point has been made. "Do you think he's documented in here some place?"

"He's probably not that rare. Stupid people attempt suicide all the time, I bet a lot of them screw it up."

"You disagree with suicide?" Ray asks as they walk into a room with bladder stones the size of softballs under a glass box.

"Not morally, but it seems weak. If you want to die, all you have to do is wait long enough."

Ray laughs, they realize the rest of the room is full of awkward portraits of Caesarean sections, and they move to the next room.

"I've thought about it," Ray says. "Sometimes life almost bores me to death, literally. I might think about it again if this next crime goes wrong, and people find out."

"Don't lie to me, you'd love being famous for murder."

"I don't want to be famous for botching one though, so no gunshot survivals, and no mistakes, otherwise it'll have to be pathetic, weak Suicide City for me."

Noah smiles and quotes, "The thought of suicide is a great consolation: by means of it one gets through many a bad night."

"Nietzsche died in an asylum with nobody to mumble at but his Nazi sister, he should have chosen suicide on one of those dark nights, there's got to be more dignity in that than a bunch of strokes."

"Maybe," Noah says. He has yet to really consider suicide himself, since he doubts his mother ever did, and she had a lot more reasons than both Noah and Ray put together.

"So what, we'll have to kidnap the kid first, that's what you're saying?"

"I don't know a better way to stay unseen during all this."

"So we swoop down and snatch him into a car or something?"

"Not a car owned by us or anyone we know, in case someone remembers it being in the area."

"That's going to be a pain to figure out."

"If it was easy everyone would do it," Noah says. Now they're in a room with a seated skeleton festooned with veins, illustrating the human circulatory system.

"I think it'll be worth it," Ray says, crouching down to get a close look at this exhibit, fogging the glass with his breath. Noah doesn't say anything until Ray looks up at him with that peaceful face he gets when he's got something to genuinely look forward to. If only he could feel like that his whole life, his pretty face would never wrinkle. "Don't you think so?"

"I must, right? Since I'm doing it with you."

Ray claps Noah's calf lightly before standing up. They've got more knowledge to gain.

3

RAY IS THE ONLY GROWN SON home for the holidays this year, so he gets to put the menorah topper on the Christmas tree, an honor always reserved for the oldest kid around. Poor youngest, Tommy, has never even touched it.

Ray and Tommy get the most generic matching gifts—the same design of sweater, one big and one small; new leather wallets with their initials embossed on them, RAK and TAK; hundred-dollar gift certificates so they can buy whatever they actually want themselves online; stockings stuffed with the same amount of matching candy. Gift giving is over in less than ten minutes. Ray gives Tommy all his candy sight unseen, which actually makes the boy feel rich indeed. Ray is old enough to find his brother's youth charming, so eighteen years really does make an adult.

Watching Tommy obsess over his sweet loot that evening—watching him hoard and organize and even stash some of it for rediscovery later—gives Ray the best gift of his life: a shimmering new idea for the ultimate crime.

Ray dashes from the house so fast on Christmas day, his shoes are untied and his jacket is only half on, but even the dry smack of Chicago's winter air doesn't bother him. He could survive naked on Mount Everest for the distance between his house and Noah's, and it just makes his time inside the front door faster. He knocks and enters without permission, calls out a hello to Mr. Kaplan and identifies himself as he steps out of his shoes and flings his jacket at the coat rack. He didn't even bring his keys or his wallet with him! He's in an ecstasy of excitement. He almost trips trying to run up the stairs three at a time, an act of physicality that should only be attempted by Olympians, not a frenzied member of the civilian class.

Ray grabs Noah into a spinning hug as he emerges from his room to investigate all the noise. Ray waltzes a surprised Noah back into his room before he whispers the word right into his ear: *"Ransom!"*

"Really?" Noah says, pleasantly surprised enough by getting carried over a threshold that he isn't criticizing Ray's idea yet, he's just hearing it.

"If we're already going to kidnap and murder," Ray says as quietly as he possibly can, his voice shaking with the effort not to shout this latest epiphanic thought everywhere. "Let's try for a ransom! I mean the problem with kidnappings for ransom is a still-living victim who can escape, remember your face or voice, all kinds of shit, this would be *the perfect crime.* It would even lead the cops away with motive, right? Because they'd be looking for people who need money, junkies or gamblers or whatever, *never* at guys like us."

"Look at you, you look like you're full of movie-quality Christmas spirit."

"But what do you think?" Ray says, his volume rising now that he's no longer using the red flag words that could implicate them if overheard.

"I think we should go for a walk," Noah says, gathering his things and dressing for the weather in a calm and orderly fashion. He notices but does not comment on the frantic bee-line path Ray left in the thin snowfall on the Kaplan's front yard (Ray did not find time to take the footpath up to the door), and they start following Ray's tracks as they stroll and Noah thinks.

Ray occupies himself by letting his surroundings dazzle him: the twinkling stars, the pure whiteness of the snow, the way the air feels so huge when the cold keeps moisture out of it. It's a big, bright world tonight!

They pass an undeveloped lot, and the icy crunch of their footsteps disturbs some creature, which causes Noah to finally speak (he classifies in rote, automatic habit).

"Eastern Screech Owl," he says, not necessarily to Ray, but just out loud.

"It sounds like a neighing horse."

"Kind of misnamed, isn't it? There's nothing screeching about that musical trill." The bird burbles at them again, perhaps a farewell as they continue past the copse of trees where it's sitting.

"Ransom," Ray says again. "It makes things a little more complicated, we'd have to contact the family, police *will* be brought into that, even if we tell them not to tell the cops, but what a success that would be. You can spend the money on your Europe trip, I'll take mine to Canada or Mexico or Indiana or something, who cares, just so long as it's outside the state, right? What do you want, five thousand, ten thousand? Take how much sounds right to you, double it, and that's what we'll ask for."

"Okay, yeah, we'll add that stuff to the list of details to figure out."

"So you're in? We're officially going for a ransom too?"

"Yes, officially," Noah says sarcastically. "I'll rubberstamp your forehead when we get back if that would reassure you."

They turn onto Ray's street and pass the decorated yard of his Jewish Christian neighbors. They can't be lazily Christian like his vaguely Catholic mother; they've got the zeal of the converted. Ray doesn't remember if their yard was lit up when he tore out of his house (he was one hundred percent in his own world at that moment), but it's certainly a beacon now—lights wrapping every tree that's theirs and festooning a manger that has baby Jesus nestled in the center.

"Hey, want to practice a dry run of this kidnap?" Ray leans close to Noah to ask, his breath tickling Noah's neck in a way that makes him shiver and flinch. "Let's go see if Jesus is attached to his hay box."

"I'd rather just do the murder; you know how Christians can get about their religious crap. Kill their kid, go to Joliet, take their tacky plastic Lord, end up in Guantanamo."

That observation makes Ray laugh so hard, he nearly kneels down in an attempt to keep his sides from splitting open.

4

NOAH VISITS RAY'S HOUSE to revisit their victimology. With ransom thrown into the fray, they can't choose a boy at random anymore, they have to pick a kid whose parents have money, and seem soft enough towards that particular kid to hand it over in the hopes of getting him back.

This task is such a cold-blooded form of math that it empowers Noah to spend time in the unwelcoming Klein house without total discomfort. Ray's parents still don't like Noah, they never really did, Ray's older brothers have counseled Ray against him, and even Tommy (who still agrees with Ray on just about everything) is ruffled by Noah, sort of like how a particularly loyal pet will dislike someone that subtracts from its owner's affections. Ray is playing a video game with Tommy when Noah arrives, ledger in hand, ready to take accounting of all the neighborhood boys; when Ray gets up to tend to Noah instead, letting his character die and mess up Tommy's mission or quest or whatever, Tommy glares at Noah with a pure and all-consuming distaste.

"Sorry," Noah mumbles at Tommy.

"Yeah, you are," Tommy says, turning back to the TV. Ray is delighted at the way his nine-year-old brother just managed to insult the only guy he knows with a genius IQ, and his laugh soothes Tommy's jealousy. At least everyone else is happy.

They ascend to Ray's barren room, decorated only with a mess of clothes, an overflowing ashtray near the window he steps out onto the roof through to follow the 'no smoking in the house' rule, and his telescope, which is what they're headed for.

"You know, the closer we choose this victim, the better vantage-point I'll have for the fallout," Ray says as he sits behind his telescope, happy at the thought of watching a funeral procession from the comfort of his own bedroom, probably.

"Also the better chance you have to become a suspect."

"You're a suspect if you're hanging around a crime where you don't belong, but I live in this neighborhood, I have a right to be concerned for the safety of its children. Just think of my little brother!"

When Ray says this, both he and Noah do think of Tommy, watching each other cautiously, in total mental synchronicity. They *did* convene to discuss the young sons of rich parents . . . isn't that what Tommy Klein is?

Ray has half a smile on his face, feeling that pure thrill of danger one feels when considering doing something truly drastic. He couldn't do that, or could he? He seems to decide he could at least talk about it.

"Who's going to actually say it first?" Ray asks.

"You just spoke, you said it first," Noah says, finally setting his notebook and pencil case down and sitting on the desktop beside them.

"Let's both talk about it," Ray says, getting comfortable for the storytelling feeling these meetings have started to take on.

"You like Tommy too much," Noah says.

"You don't. And you're not the only one who can train himself to be beyond the reaches of emotion. I'll be killing somebody's beloved little brother, so why shouldn't I do it to mine? Wouldn't that be fair?"

"Not to the rest of your family."

"I like all of them less than Tommy."

"That argument is a Gordian knot, and besides, all the practical concerns we've already figured out are way too complicated if you're part of the victim's family."

"How? I don't need a car, it'll be easy to lure him."

"If you lure him, people know you were in charge of him, you would be the last person to see him alive, you would be the main suspect, your parents would blame you forever—"

"All right, all right," Ray says, cutting Noah off.

"You couldn't help with any of the ransom stuff after the disappearance of Tommy, you'd actually have to leave all that to me, and I don't want it, and you do, so—"

"You're going to make a great lawyer, you can't stop arguing even after you've won."

Noah finally stops talking. That was a little backhanded and self-serving, but it was still a compliment based on observable facts. Noah's face does the opposite of a blush—his blood rushes away from the skin to somewhere else. He picks up his ledger to hide it.

"Start listing names, I'll write them down in Sanskrit, we'll discuss, and burn the page before I leave."

"Very cloak-and-dagger," Ray says, putting his eye to the telescope. "Okay, Levine, Johnny. Adelman, William. Schaffer, Kendall. The Wallaces have a bunch of grandkids, we could go for one of them." The list goes on until every family on the block with a young heir is represented. Then they start crossing off names.

Some fathers are too stingy, some are wealthy but not liquid, Ray is thinning down the list with an abundance of gossip he's picked up from his mother. He knows more about their neighbors than Noah knows about the other members of his own family. In the end their list is short enough to remember: Danny, Johnny, Henry, and an open mind in case a better opportunity presents himself when the time comes. Noah asks for Ray's lighter to destroy this first piece of physical evidence they've produced, and Ray hands it over before digging a bottle of whiskey out of an overstuffed decorative pillow on the tiny bench seat under his smoking window.

"To the perfect crime," he toasts, taking a swig and handing it to Noah. Noah also raises the bottle in a small salute, and takes his own sip. The burn of the liquor numbs his lips too much; when Ray rewards Noah for his work today with a peck on the lips at the moment of departure, Noah barely feels it.

5

Spring finally arrives in the Midwest, and with it comes an American urge for a road trip.

Ray hasn't spared much thought on how to acquire a car for the commission of their crime without using his name (seems like something Noah will figure out first), but since it's agreed that a car will be involved in the kidnapping, he has begun to think about the route of body transport. The faster the actual murder is completed, the better, less of a chance for fight or flight from the victim . . . but then there's a dead body in the car for who knows how many miles of highway. Problematic, that.

In February, on their mutually dateless Valentine's Day, Ray brings up the question of body disposal, and Noah suggests a dump site: a remote area of Hegewisch just over the state line of Indiana he knows from his birding classes. A lot to love about that idea! The body probably won't be found in some nowhere drain pipe, and even if it is, it becomes an Indiana body, not an Illinois one, and certainly far from a Chicago corpse. Perfect, but . . . they still have to get the body from Chicago to that culvert.

In March, Ray demands a daytrip, a dry run, a dress rehearsal. He wants to know how long it takes to drive from their neighborhood to this pipe Noah knows about, and what it feels like to drag a body over to its final resting place. Ray asks Tommy how much he weighs and packs a suitcase five pounds heavier to use as their mock-body. Ray tells Noah he's driving, since Ray will have to be in back where the action's going to happen. Noah wholeheartedly agrees.

The day starts out so optimistically.

"This is about a thirty-minute drive," Noah says as they get into his car for the trip with snacks, drinks, a stopwatch, that fucking ledger book Noah's keeping for notes on this crime which will soon have to be burned with their victim's clothes, the murder weapon, everything but the money and the memory. "I usually push the speed limit with my birding students, but we can't break any more laws than the ones we're already planning that day."

"Yeah, it's smart to keep the lawlessness to a minimum," Ray says, feeling the purr of Noah's upstarting engine through his toes, his viscera (as Noah refers to guts), his teeth. He's vibrating with energy, watching the timer reflect the passing sky, which starts out as a fluffy panorama of cloudscape, but slowly starts to curdle into a storm.

Thirty minutes for traffic and safety becomes more like forty minutes due to inclement weather conditions, with the road turned black and slick and the other drivers igniting their headlights for visibility through the water.

"We'll just budget a whole hour for this leg of the journey," Noah tries to reassure Ray. "We'll have all day for this, it's no problem."

But it is a problem, and Ray wishes he'd sat in the back for this test drive instead of the passenger seat, because though there might be a diminished sense of adventure in the back seat on the practice run, at least he would have been able to hide from Noah's concerned glances. The traffic is one thing, the weather another, but complications keep arising even after the rain lets up: there's construction on I-90.

The traffic is whittled down to one lane for a time, with concrete barriers scraping along one side, and orange plastic netting designating the work site on the other. Sitting in the passenger seat, Ray knows for sure that the workers are close enough to the car to roll down the window and shake hands, make friends. One of the guys actually jaywalks between the cars to cross the street. Might as well let people press their faces up to the glass, since that's the only way they could see more clearly what's in the back seat.

"This isn't going to work," Ray says. They can't have a body in the backseat and drive through here. All his shivering excitement drains from him in an instant.

"We can take I-94 instead," Noah suggests. "We'll plan ahead for a day without rain. We can put the body in the trunk?"

"We're killing him in the car, so that means somewhere we'd have to stop and drag it out in the open. Maybe pick a boy that would actually fit in that suitcase," Ray murmurs, looking back at their representative cargo. "Or get a car where you can access the trunk from inside the cab, those exist."

"You know," Noah says slowly, "this is what I worry about the most."

"Getting caught with a dead body? No shit, that's what we're both worried about, it would worry anyone."

"No," Noah says as they pull out of the tight squeeze of the construction zone, which gives him the freedom to look over at Ray for a longer moment, with a horribly adult expression of disappointment on his face. "I worry about your morale. This hasn't even happened yet and you're already so down. I worry that we'll do this, and right away it'll be like that drive back from the ZBT house, on a much more serious scale."

"But I'll have so much to look forward to," Ray says, remembering his solo return to his frat house. There will be a real investigation for a missing child, focus, attention. It'll be all over the news, and Ray will get to watch that news with his mother, with his brother, with a consuming sense of power and superiority to those who wonder at what he's actually done. "It won't be the same."

"Not the same, no," Noah agrees. "Worse."

Ray sighs, not liking how true that sounds. Noah flips the turn signal and moves into the right lane, and leaves it on as they approach an upcoming rest stop. He's pulling over.

"Don't stop," Ray says, the closest thing to a plea he's ever made. "The timer's still going, and I want to see this pipe place you know about, and this drive is just the first collection of data, right? To find out how much we don't know, haven't thought of yet, so we can plan accordingly. Besides—"

"Yeah, Ray," Noah says gently. "I'm not stopping you."

6

THOUGH RAY PERKS UP ONCE he sees that culvert—its cavernous maw and the murky weeds in the water below it—Noah doesn't find any renewal there. Ray starts taking in deep gulps of country air (nevermind that the ditch water smells kind of sour), and galloping around trying to see the opening of the pipe from every angle to reassure himself that yes, this must be the place. Meanwhile Noah thinks of how peaceful he finds bird watching, alone, in silence, in empty places like this, and wonders if leaving a dead body out here will taint the closest thing he has to a spiritual communion. Noah thinks of his mother without missing her when he goes birding. This little project of Ray's better not ruin that.

The drive home is quicker, and Ray completely resurfaces from his pessimism by the time they get back. Noah can't shake a sense of pity out of himself for a much longer time. Not when he grabs a snack before dinner, not the next day when he smirks at completing the paperwork needed for housing, class registration, and a meal plan at Harvard, not when he sees Ray a few days after that to listen to him prattle on about cars and drive times and plans to make that lackluster trip *again*, just for the research. Noah can't even pretend to listen after the first five minutes. Ray realizes he's talking to himself after another ten minutes pass. Noah's staring at him from a very remote place inside of his own mind.

"Hey, who died?" Ray asks, thinking he's being funny and that a joke like that can break the tension. "Why do you look so glum?"

They're sitting in the living room of Noah's house, and Noah stands up from his seat on the couch with an urge to flee to the woods, but he doesn't want to actually leave Ray's company, and doesn't have the words to describe that feeling of push and pull at the same time. He goes upstairs instead, knowing Ray will follow him (out of curiosity if not concern), and when they're behind his bedroom door, Noah kisses him hard. It's less of a kiss and more of a way to press their lips together between two sets of teeth, an attempt to squeeze all that useless verbiage right out of them.

"Hey," Ray says, offended that he was given no warning maybe, or perhaps Noah has bad breath and doesn't realize it. Noah glares at him regardless of the reason. His part of the deal is not harder to endure than Noah's, and it's offensive for him to act otherwise.

Noah pushes him lightly towards the bed, mostly because a real push would probably start a fight he would lose, he's that annoyed right now. Ray rolls his eyes, but complies. All he has to do is ignore what's happening, he doesn't have to participate. It's not that big a burden.

Ray gets into position, pants down, underwear up, eyes closed, and a hand covering them like he's suddenly got a splitting headache. Noah wants a step further than this. He pulls down everything before joining Ray on the bed, and starts to tug down Ray's underwear too. That makes him break his spell, and turn towards Noah with 'no' stamped all over his face. Noah puts his hand over Ray's mouth and assures him, "I'm not doing that, just ... don't."

Ray squints warily at Noah, then at the hand still touching his face, then he turns back away from it. A little trust, at last; that's nice.

Noah puts himself between Ray's legs, nothing drastic, nothing more than the same sort of friction they've shared before, but this time with direct skin contact, a space to thrust into, and because of that, a florid heat ... it's over faster than ever. Ray scrambles to the bathroom as fast as he can. Noah sits up, buttons up, and waits. Ray comes back in wiping his hands dry on his hair, swiping it into a helmet formation.

"Do you feel better now?" he asks.

Noah shrugs. Sort of, but not really. "Maybe a little bit relieved."

Ray snorts at the choice of word, but that's something Noah likes about Ray: he can take his licks in good humor.

"You're still up for this aren't you?" Ray asks. "I know it's like, not the most fun you've ever had, but you won't quit on me."

Noah shakes his head. "Wither thou goest, I will go."

"Okay. I'm going to lunch, wither thou goest for a burger with me?"

"Yeah, sure," Noah says, standing and moving before the answer can even reach his mouth. "And you mis-conjugated nearly everything you just said."

"I promise to talk about something we both find boring as shit, so it's fair," Ray says as they descend the stairs.

"The weather?"

"You'll turn talking about weather into talking about birds somehow. How about books?"

"You don't read enough. Politics?"

"Too close to law. How about our friends' relationships and who will break up first?"

"Your friends," Noah corrects, "but yes, that sounds boring enough."

"There, you see that? We can accomplish anything when we work together, you and I."

"That didn't last long, I already want you to shut up."

"Good luck getting what you want, I don't think it'll happen."

"That's the problem with all your friends' relationships right there," Noah says as he locks the front door behind them and steps out into the most obnoxiously happy spring day. "They want what they can't have, but no one's honest enough to admit it."

When that observation makes Ray laugh, Noah finally starts to feel better.

7

THE DAY RAY TRUSTS THAT he'll actually go through with taking a life is the day he finds his ride to the finish line. Some guy he knew from a study group that eventually stopped telling Ray when the meetings were (Ray did not take studying seriously and insisted on being a distraction) mentions to him when they pass each other at the registrar's office that he and some buddies were going on a long camping trip near the Canadian border. Something about hiking trails, kayaking around the boundary waters, returning to nature. Ray lets this guy chatter about his fetish for flint lighters and dehydrated food for nearly half an hour, just so he can take in the opportunity that's presenting itself to him: this kid has a car. His friends might have cars. Those cars will be unattended while they're away camping. Those cars are not associated with himself or with Noah.

"That sounds awesome," Ray says to . . . Paul! That's his name. "Like real survivalist mountain man stuff. Let me buy you a beer before you leave." Paul agrees to that, and Ray means to get him that beer, but first he has to do some shopping. He needs a key impression thingy, and a cover story for getting access to Paul's keys. He overnight orders a keychain—a perfect gift!

But that's not all he gets for this covert mission. The key impression kit is the least of it (apparently the container with the clay or silicon for the impression is called a 'clam shell'—Noah will like that—and what a pearl it will contain). Get the impression, take it to a hardware store, have the key made, not a problem. Here's the problem: which car does that key belong to, and where will it be when it when Ray needs it?

Ray does research all night, and finds a GPS tracking device for a car, magnetic so he can slap it on the car's frame without being noticed, with a long battery life and an ability to locate it through his phone. Now to execute the best idea Ray's ever had, and attempt to answer every question Noah has before the guy even gets a chance to ask them. He sets up that beer meeting with Paul.

Ray's talent for talk has never served him better than it does this last Friday in April. He starts off with, "Tell me all about this trip, man, how'd you decide to do it?"

He lets Paul say anything and everything he wants, moving his face into surprise and happiness shapes, listening all the while for any information he can use. They're flying up to Maine and disembarking from there on their trek (so the car does stay here), and the dates specifically are May 10-25 (so that's the window of opportunity; good weather for it). He buys Paul beer until the guy has to pee, and when he gets up for the bathroom, Ray finally goes into action.

"Hey, leave your keys, I have a surprise for you." Paul looks at him, dumb and confused, or maybe it's just the backwards baseball hat that makes him look like that. "Trust me," Ray says, "it's a surprise, not a prank." And Paul does trust him. Idiot.

Ray gets two impressions of the car key first (two just in case one gets fucked up), hiding his task under the table of their booth. The key reveals it's for a Ford of some sort, and Ray checks to see that the ridges are clear in both molds before he safely pockets the clam shells. Next he pulls out a carabineer keychain with a bunch of cutesy wilderness features on it and starts to attach this to the bundle. His furtive movements with his friend's keys will look totally innocent now!

"What are you doing?" Paul asks when he returns.

"Getting outsmarted by a key ring," Ray says. "There, I got you something for your trip."

Carabineer for mountain climbing or whatever, plus a thermometer, a compass, "and you know what that is, right?" Ray asks as Paul oohs and ahhs over his trinket. "That's a bottle opener. I'm sure I don't have to tell you what to do with that."

Paul's had enough beers to give Ray a hug over this gift. Ray finds this very satisfying; he can be anyone's Casanova when he wants to be.

One task left: get the tracker onto that vehicle. They walk out into the parking lot after drinking some responsible but sink-tasting bar water, and Ray goes into his last manipulation.

"Sure you're okay to drive?" Yes, Paul says he's okay to drive.

"What's that you're driving?" It's a Ford Fusion. Ray's heart starts to squirm as he looks at the back seat.

"Do those seats fold down?" Yeah, you can almost crawl into the trunk from the back seat. Paul opens the back door and pulls down the seat to illustrate this. When Ray bends down to look, he palms the tracker onto the bottom of the car.

"Hmm, this would be a terrible car to kidnap somebody with, they could jump right out at you!" Ray couldn't resist.

8

NOAH TRIES TO POKE HOLES in Ray's car theft idea, but none of them really hold up. It's a horrible thing to admit, but Ray figured out a nice little plan, all things considered. He says maybe they should put a different license plate on it, but that's easier to spot by the authorities than leaving it alone, Noah knows it himself. He says to Ray, what if the parking spot they take it from is in use when they come back? Because then Paul might suspect something, check the mileage? But even he isn't that paranoid, and Noah's met Paul; that kid probably forgets where he parked his car once a week. The trunk access is a really good idea, Ray can pick up the car wearing a lot of disguising clothing (the clothes they each wear that day will be burned anyway) and sunglasses and a hat. Minimize what they touch, wipe their prints, tarp in the trunk to put the body on . . . intellectually it all stands up, but it makes Noah's knees weak with dread. He can't name a sound reason to stop these wheels from rolling unless he cops to cowardice, and he can't (won't) do that. Ray assigns the third week in May as the date of the crime. By the second week in May, they've collected everything else they need, their supplies. Ray repeats the list several times, reassuring them both that it's everything, they really have thought of everything.

One: cash for the day in all small denominations so if they pass a toll, stop for food, need to buy something they forgot, they don't leave a paper trail.

Two: they've got many weapons that don't necessarily look suspicious until they're used to cause harm (a length of rope in case of strangulation, a heavy chisel with the blade taped up for bludgeoning, even a small syringe to induce an air bubble into their victim—that's Noah's preferred method, but this is Ray's thing, and he wants to take more action than that).

Three: they've got letters printed up from that laptop they stole out of the

ZBT house (they'll take a hammer to the hard drive and throw the whole mess off a bridge ... after).

Four: a burner cell for phone calls to communicate the details of the ransom (the letters are purposefully vague to keep the cops out of the action as long as possible). The letters and phone calls will send the boy's father on a relay with the money, ending with him tossing it from a train—Ray and Noah will collect it and flee before the cops can swarm, but that's a whole other day's list.

Five: alibis prepared carefully so that they can never be confirmed or unconfirmed, saying they spent the day (together or apart depending on when they're asked) in crowded places without surveillance. They're ready. Ray is excited.

"Let's celebrate!" Ray demands on the Friday before the big week, clapping both hands on Noah's face to guarantee he says yes. They will take the car around their neighborhood every day Monday through Thursday in between their obligations (Noah's morning classes, Ray's nightly social life) and wait for the first opportunity to snatch a boy on their list, or any boy like those. The ransom letter is addressed *Dear Sir*, so any boy with a wealthy father will do, as long as he separates from the flock and flies close enough to Ray's grasp.

They must eat, drink, and be merry, for come next week, somebody dies.

They start drinking at the pub on campus, actually called The Pub, which causes Noah to explain the origin of the word and the nature of public houses in England. He does this once when sober, in an attempt to fill the awkward silence of what starts as a very tepid and doomed celebration while Ray digs a fingernail into a crack in the bar top, waiting for him to stop. Noah tells his story again when he is drunk, assuming Ray wasn't listening the first time and getting into deeper detail, gesturing with his hands, which is a great indicator of his inebriation. Noah attempts to tell it a third time when he is so plastered that he doesn't remember the first two tries. Ray does remember them, and slurs at Noah to shut the fuck up.

They spend about four hours drinking and talking about anything but what they're both thinking. The awkward stares and clear overhearing that start to happen once they're so drunk they're drawing attention eventually urge them to leave. They've been here a dozen times, but still manage to get turned around trying to find their way out of the hallway this campus pub is located in. The Pub tries to look old-timey; the linoleum and florescent lights and air ducts in the hallway do not. It's like walking out of a stage set into the real, grimy, over-lit world. That divide doesn't bother Noah very much tonight, that's what enough alcohol and the right company can do for a person.

They walk towards the train stop; they're too drunk to wander between campus and home, especially at night when the South Side's reputation asserts itself the strongest. Even so, as soon as they step off campus into the real world, a man is at the station's entrance trying to panhandle them. Ray and Noah move past him and his swears at their disregard, through the stiles and up the stairs, where Ray starts giggling and panhandling the other people on the platform in imitation. Some move away from him, but a few others roll their eyes and shake their heads in mild amusement, like he's their own weird nephew or something. Maybe that's because there's more light on the platform than below it, and light makes everyone feel safe. Maybe it's the fact that Ray can't even catch his breath through his laughter to seem in need. One person he bothers even helps Ray when he starts to overbalance near the tracks.

"Hey, watch your friend," the lady scolds to Noah. Noah collects Ray and puts them both on a bench.

"You know," Ray says after he regains his breath and looks around like he's basking at this crumby Green Line stop, relishing it, "if I ever have to kill you, because you'll be my only living witness after this and it's the smart thing to do, I'll probably push you into a train."

"I've felt you thinking about that more than once," Noah says. "Your face is a lot more readable than you think it is."

"Then why do you ever let me stand behind you when a train approaches? You got a death wish?"

Noah shrugs, and doesn't answer, since Ray's already gabbling on about something else. Ray's the one with the death wish, Noah just likes to make him happy.

9

It's Tuesday night, and as Ray reviews the last two days' events, he finds reason to be optimistic about tomorrow.

The first day out shopping for a victim was Monday, and he and Noah were both in agreement that there was no rush on Monday. They took turns driving, getting comfortable with the placement of the car's buttons and levers, with the migration patterns of the kids from school to parks to homes on sidewalks and shortcuts. Noah had his birding binoculars with them, for back seat use only through the tinted windows. People would probably notice two guys scoping out a playground through binoculars and get all inquisitive. Monday was a peaceful little outing, full of promise. Plenty of boys they knew were out, plenty of boys they didn't know were off by themselves here and there . . . eventually the right boy would find his way to them.

Tuesday did not start out as low pressure as Monday. Ray definitely hoped that Tuesday could be the day, and Noah feared the same thing. It put some static between them. They argued about whether or not the radio should be on (Ray said why not, and Noah said any song they heard was just going to remind them of what they did this day, and Ray asked what was so bad about that, and Noah scoffed at him and looked longingly away and out the window). It was an uncomfortable ride after that disagreement, but they parted on okay terms. After a day of fruitless searching, they left the car on campus grounds and walked home together through the evening air.

"The next rich kid we spot alone we have to take," Ray told Noah. "There can't be any hesitating. If not tomorrow, and if not Thursday, then we've lost our window and it'll never happen."

"What a tragedy that would be," Noah griped, and Ray just stared at him as they kept strolling. The longer Noah's silence stretched, the more a profound disappointment started to well up in Ray, the sort of sorrow that is only felt when a person suspects the goodbye they're saying might be the last one of its kind.

Noah finally met Ray's gaze, and nearly flinched from it.

"Good grief, don't look at me like that, you look like a kicked puppy."

"You really hope this doesn't work out," Ray told him. "You want to look back at this week and think 'ha ha, so funny, that week I went joyriding for no reason,' and you'd have no regrets."

"You say that like you're giving me news I don't already have," Noah told him, fighting back in his sarcastic little way. It's kind of bitchy, if Ray really thinks about it, the same way his mother wins fights, by aggressively surrendering.

"If we get a real opportunity, and miss it because you drag your feet, I will never speak to you again."

"No dithering or shilly-shallying, I got it."

"Shilly-shall..." Ray repeated in a daze of trying to interpret a term he may have never actually heard in his life. "I should really just kill you, it would save us both a lot of trouble."

"That is true," Noah agreed with a sigh as they approached their splitting place. "Too bad you like me too much."

"Tomorrow or Thursday," Ray said as sternly as possible. "I'm serious."

"Until then," Noah said with a wave, and Ray waved back to show that he had no hard feelings . . . yet.

Now Ray is sitting out on his roof, smoking cigarettes and drinking some cheap Canadian whiskey from a squeezy bottle with a crazy straw built into the cap, something he found in the back of a kitchen cabinet last year and keeps with his booze stash. It's probably a leftover from his own boyhood. There's not much that's young in the house anymore, outside of Tommy, and that kid gets older every day, as one might expect. This could be the last night of Ray's childhood, truly, and for someone who's been forced to stay young and infantilized no matter what he did or how many responsibilities he took on, Ray is happy to drink a toast to its death. Down with kid stuff, up with crime! Cheers to that.

He retreats back into his room when his cigarettes are gone and there's nothing left to distract him from the night's chill. He'll keep drinking, stay busy, until he's finally tired enough to sleep without patience. Lay out tomorrow's outfit, take a shower, clean the taste of cigarettes out of his mouth because he hates waking up with it, lie down to fantasize about actually choking the life out of someone, and finally fall asleep in that position, with both hands behind his head, like a comfortable man in a hammock, on vacation and at peace.

10

It doesn't take his ill-used field glasses to tell that Noah feels sick on the morning of May twenty-first. It's the first thing Ray says to him when he pulls out of the parking lot to where Noah is waiting just beyond view of the campus security cams. He gets out and hands Noah the keys and says, "You look like you want to puke."

Noah just nods and gets into the driver's seat. That is true. It's been true all week.

Ray gets into the back seat, binoculars in his lap for a quick draw if he needs a closer look, and Noah drives in increasing circles around the school buildings as the bells ring and the kids disgorge and their packs thin out towards home.

Ray keeps up a stream of color commentary as Noah chauffeurs him around, identifying kids and listing every single fact he knows about their families. Whenever they notice a kid moving alone, the boy suddenly turns a corner, or walks near some loitering adult, or checks a mailbox meaning he's home (and courteous). Ray notices a kickball game forming as they begin their second pass through the school zone, this time driving east to west through the streets instead of circling. Noah parks the car under a shady tree so they can both scope in comfort from the edge of the park's playing field. Ray fishes a sandwich baggie of trail mix out of his pocket and holds it between the two of them, offering. Noah snacks on the pretzels and peanuts, leaves the candy and fruit to Ray.

"If it was up to choice, which one would you want to kill?" Ray asks, making chitchat.

"Whoever that kid sticking his finger in the other kid's face is, he once shot me with a rubber band gun, him I wouldn't mind seeing dead. What about you?"

"I don't think I actually care. They're all the same to me."

The bossy one Noah pointed out makes himself a team captain. A girl tries to join in the game and is rebuffed. She leaves alone, but a lot of good that does Ray and Noah, since they're only looking for boys. One kid takes a spectacular spill and starts limping home, but his friend is helping him, or at least sticking near him for moral if not physical support. The game is nowhere near over at that point, but with two players departing, everyone but Bossy gives up. He yells his face red, but he can't influence any of the others to keep playing. His lack of control makes him kick the ball into the trees in anger. He turns towards the school, probably looking for more people to shout at. The rest wander towards the sidewalks.

"You're right," Ray says as they return to their cruising positions to follow the dispersal. "That kid *is* a little shit. Too bad he'd probably be impossible to trick into the car."

"Yes, that's quite a pity."

One block away a boy is finally walking alone, but when they pull up close to him, Noah accidentally hits the power locks instead of the window down button and speeds back up in a flustered panic.

"Noah, what the fuck?" Ray scolds him, watching out the back window as their big opportunity fades into the distance. "What the fuck did I tell you *yesterday*, man, what the hell is wrong with you?"

"Ray, pay attention to what's in front of you," Noah says, because the next right turn reveals another lone boy, on a side street instead of in front of everyone's living room windows, and this boy they both know.

"Robbie Rosen," whispers Ray, sitting up straight and rigid, like a bloodhound with a scent.

"He must be visiting his grandparents or something," Noah says, seeing no one on the street before them, and no one but Ray in the rearview mirror. His pupils are dilated and his breaths small and shallow.

"Yeah, something like that, probably," Ray agrees, and he grazes Noah's neck with his fingernails as he leans over the center console to hit the window down button on the passenger side himself.

"You know what that kid is?" Noah asks, then answers, because this is a set-up and not a real question. "He's a group of crows."

Ray laughs, and the friendliest smile lights up his face. That will go a long way towards convincing Robbie to go for a ride.

"I know why that's funny," Ray says, victorious and pleased all the way to his core.

"I don't," Noah says honestly, but he eases the car up to Robbie and leaves the charm offensive to Ray. It turns out Noah really will do anything for him.

ABOUT THE AUTHOR

L.A. FIELDS is the author of The Disorder Series, the short story collection *Countrycide*, and *My Dear Watson*, a queer Sherlock Holmes pastiche. Her work has appeared in anthologies of horror, erotica, and academia.

She has a BA in English Literature from the New College of Florida, and an MFA in Creative Writing - Fiction from Columbia College Chicago. She lives in Dallas, TX with a cat and a day job.

CPSIA information can be obtained
at www.ICGtesting.com
Printed in the USA
FFOW02n1212120616
24850FF

9 781590 216262